The Hawksbill Crag

By

Richard Oliver Snelson

Copyright © 2011 by Richard Oliver Snelson

Cover Photograph by
Copyright © 2009 - Derrald Farnsworth-Livingston, Journey of Light Photography
www.journeyoflight.com

Cover Design by Connie Luebbert
www.saltandlight-studios.com
Art director/owner

Edited by Diana Ross, Copy Editor for *The Ozark Mountaineer*

Introduction by Dr. Fred Roger Pfister, Editor at *The Ozark Mountaineer*

ISBN 0-7414-6523-X

Printed in the United States of America

Published May 2011

INFINITY PUBLISHING
1094 New DeHaven Street, Suite 100
West Conshohocken, PA 19428-2713
Toll-free (877) BUY BOOK
Local Phone (610) 941-9999
Fax (610) 941-9959
Info@buybooksontheweb.com
www.buybooksontheweb.com

Early Reader's Review of The Hawksbill Crag.

Rich Snelson has a natural aptitude for capturing the very essence of a bygone era. I found myself swallowed up in Captain Paintier's tribulations, his burning desire to right a wrong that occurred when he was a boy of 16—the beating and hanging of an innocent little black girl. The guilt that follows him through his adult life for not trying to save her spurs him to write a book about the egregious miscarriage of justice.

The book becomes a threat to Senator Saunders who is campaigning for governor. If the truth about him should surface, his career would be shattered. There are a few who want Paintier dead, making for a very exciting and suspenseful read. Along with danger, floods, graphic shootouts reminiscent of John Wayne, Paintier finds true love with Ruth Anne Gordon, a genteel southern school teacher. The reader will be drawn in by Nelson Paintier's tall good looks, his integrity and devotion to a principle. Tony Hillerman devotees will love The Hawksbill Crag.

— D. H. Clair - Creator of "The Infinite Writer eZine,"
author of the novel, "The House on Slocum Road."

INTRODUCTION
By: Dr. Fred R. Pfister

The Civil War in the Ozarks:
Setting the Stage For *The Hawksbill Crag*

People of my generation or older in the Ozarks perhaps remember being amazed at the standard American History textbooks of our junior high and high school days when it came to the American Civil War.

The large scale battles back East, often described in considerable detail, were much different from the skirmishes, battles, fights, and feuds in Missouri and Arkansas, as related by local historians and our neighborhood elders, telling of local incidents and events that they heard from their elders, who had lived through the very events they had related.

The variance of events in the Ozarks and back East was due to a variety of reasons: the fact that Missouri was a "border state"; that the nation in 1860 had no "Midwest" (anything west of the Mississippi was still "the West" to Easterners); that the Ozarks of southern Missouri and northern Arkansas was sparsely populated; and that the war's after-effects lingered for decades in the Ozarks after the surrender at Appomattox.

Missouri was a border state in two ways, north and south, the most obvious, but also east and west, with the Mississippi River being the dividing line. Looking back from today's perspective, battles fought in Missouri as part of the Trans-Mississippi War had little influence concerning the outcome, and because of the sparse population of the Ozarks, battles in Missouri and Arkansas pale to mere skirmishes compared to the large scale slaughter in battles back East.

In spite of having little impact on the Civil War's outcome, the Civil War had a tremendous impact on the Ozarks, and Missouri had a higher percentage of participants in the War than any other state—109,000 Union solders and 30,000 Confederate soldiers, 60 percent of all men old enough to be mustered.

At the outbreak of the war, the Ozarks was still sparsely populated, and in that sense was of little importance. The area had few strategic materials that were needed by either the Confederacy or Union, with the notable exception of the Meramec Ironworks near Saint James, which produced iron for cannonballs and James B. Eads' gunships, which were built in Saint Louis, and a number of small lead mines scattered in the southern half of the state. (Missouri's large lead deposits would not be discovered until well after the war.)

However, events in Missouri were harbingers of what was to happen back east later. Carthage, in Jasper County, was the site of the first land battle of the Civil War, July 5, 1861, preceding the first Battle of Bull Run by 16 days and Missouri's biggest battle at Wilson's Creek by more than a month.

The Ozarks area was marked by two large-scale battles. The first, Missouri's biggest, was the Battle of Wilson's Creek, southwest of Springfield on August 10, 1861. Lasting for six hours, this brief but savage encounter of Gen. Sterling Price's Confederate forces with those of the Union's Gen. Nathaniel Lyon produced

2,330 casualties. Wilson's Creek was a Confederate victory, but the Union regained control of southwest Missouri by the winter of 1862.

The second major battle in the Ozarks was at Pea Ridge, Arkansas, March 6 to 8, 1862. It was the turning point of the war in the Ozarks. After the victory at Wilson's Creek, the Confederate forces expected a victory, especially since they outnumbered their Union foes 2 to 1. The outnumbered Union forces prevailed at Pea Ridge; as a result, the Ozarks area was ostensibly under Union control.

The compelling issue of the Civil War, slavery, was not a burning issue in the Ozarks. It did not develop a slave economy. The hilly, rocky Ozarks did not support the kinds of crops, largely cotton and tobacco, grown on the Southern plantations which demanded a large labor force. Land use in the Ozarks consisted of small farms, worked by the landowner and his family within large areas of wilderness forest. The only farmers who had large holdings of slaves were those in the "Little Dixie" area along the fertile Missouri River, north of the Ozarks, and those in the bottom lands of the rivers south of the Ozarks, the Arkansas and the lower end of the White. Some Ozark families had slaves, but not many. If they did, they were frequently typical of the historical family of the eastern Missouri Ozarks and the incident at Steelville that Richard Snelson bases his novel *The Hawksbill Crag* on.

The 1860 census in Taney County showed a holding of 84 slaves spread over 24 families, with the largest owner having 10. There were 5 free Blacks. Compare that to the better farmland area of Greene County, which had 9 free Blacks and 1,668 slaves. Douglas County (named after Stephen B. Douglas) recorded no African Americans, slave or free. In fact, many Ozarkers, even into this century, lived a life during which they never laid eyes on an African American. Most Ozarkers were indifferent to the slavery issue or were generally supporters of the Confederacy. As one resident said, "Our sympathies are with the South but our interests are with the Union."

This pro-Southern leaning of the Ozarks is evidenced by the name of the Taney county seat (after John Forsyth of Georgia) and Crawford County, after Georgia Senator William H. Crawford. Taney County and the village of Taneyville were named after Roger Brooke Taney, the U.S. Supreme Court Chief Justice in the Dred Scott Decision of 1857. Though the county had been named for him 20 years earlier, there was no outcry to change the county name.

In a region that today is staunchly conservative and in which most residents are registered with "the party of Lincoln" as voters, one finds it difficult to conceive that 150 years ago, voters looked with disfavor on Abraham Lincoln, his policies, and the new Republican Party. In fact, in the four slave states which did not secede (Missouri, Kentucky, Maryland, and Delaware), Lincoln came in fourth in every state except Delaware (where he finished third). Lincoln won only two counties of 996 in those four states, both in Missouri. In fact, residents of Greene County were shocked when Lincoln polled 42 votes in the 1860 election. In the counties of Taney, Stone, Christian, Ozark and Douglas, not a single vote was cast for Lincoln. The next election produced equally lopsided results for Lincoln, largely because the Federals controlled the area, many Southern sympathizers were in the army or had been driven away, and because Union soldiers voted in local elections.

The hostilities in the Ozarks that resulted with the election of Lincoln didn't produce large-scale battles; instead, hostilities were in the form of innumerable and interminable raids, forays, and skirmishes by roaming bands of bushwhackers, much like Captain Nelson Paintier encounters in *The Hawksbill Crag*. The use of small, mobile bands of marauding irregulars was introduced by the Confederacy. Such raiders could harass the stronger Union enemy and tie up both resources and men which could be more effectively used in the more important and bigger battles east of the Mississippi.

The Missouri Ozarks, with few slaves, an indifference to the issue of slavery, and an independent people who just wanted to be left alone to hunt, trap, and till their garden and farm, was caught between two radical and passionate elements. Not far from the hills of the Ozarks is Kansas, where radical abolitionist feelings predominated, resulting in the burning of the Ozarks town of Osceola, and the equally vicious retaliatory raid on Lawrence, Kansas.

Arkansas to the south was a strong pro-Confederacy state, dominated by the numerous plantation owners of the big river valleys. The geography and the independent temperament of the Scotch-Irish who settled here had both served to isolate the Ozarks. In 1860, as the result of politics, these people and their region were caught squarely in the middle of the conflict. The Ozarks was at the mercy of roving marauders from both sides—and also to those who believed in neither faction, but used the excuse of war to raid, rape, rob and pillage.

To compound the bad situation of being caught between two forces, Indian Territory lay just west in what is now Oklahoma. It was a refuge for outlaws, vagabonds, and desperadoes of every ilk, and the no-man's land law that prevailed there allowed gangs to make hit-and-run attacks on helpless Ozark homesteads whose men had enlisted and were off to war for one side or the other. Bands of guerrillas and bushwhackers terrorized the surrounding countryside. Those who weren't killed fled in terror. Jasper County, which shared a border with Indian Territory and Kansas, serves as an example of the decimation of the area's population. In the 1860 census it counted 6,883 residents, but by the end of the war only 30 were left.

Names of desperadoes whose career may have begun during the war but frequently continued after it are legion and some became well-known beyond the region of local history and have been much written about: Frank Dalton and gang, Cole Younger, Jesse and Frank James, "Bloody Bill" Anderson. Lesser known names were Bill Watson, and Tom Livingston, gunned down, after a long career during the war, in front of the Cedar County courthouse at Stockton.

One of the "lesser knowns" is John R. Kelso, an example of a leader who was a respected citizen in peacetime but when exposed to the rigors of war became a psychopathic fanatic. Kelso was known as a scholar of languages and philosophy who became a school teacher at Ozark, but one who became an ardent Unionist and held all Confederates to be traitors, guilty of treason, and deserving death. It was said of Kelso that he could lie at the side of a road in ambush, with a Latin grammar in one hand and a cocked pistol in the other waiting for his intended Confederate sympathizer victim. He was considered modern and liberal and forced his wife and daughter to adopt the freedom-giving dress advocated by Amelia Bloomer. After the war, he was elected to Congress as a radical Republican and did all he could to thwart the president's efforts toward a rational plan of reunification and reconstruction.

Alfred Cook might be considered a pacifist bushwhacker. At the beginning of the war, Cook and his wife Rebecca and their 7 children were living on a farm north of Taneyville. Both Alfred and Rebecca were descendants of slave-holding families, and their parents had settled along Beaver and Swan creeks with their family slaves. Though probably sympathetic to the Southern cause, Cook tried to remain neutral, but foraging parties from both sides raided area farms, taking what they pleased and displeasing those from whom it was taken. Men who stayed at home might be called to the door and shot down by some fanatic of one side or another. Confederate sympathizers, or those whose loyalties were unknown, were plagued by the "Mountain Feds" scattered through the area who served as informants for the Unionists. Cook and his family, caught in the vortex of the Rebellion, faced starvation. Driven by desperation and criminal acts committed against them and their families, Cook and 13 or more others banded together for mutual protection. They adopted the tactics of their despoilers, and Cook and his followers made retaliatory raids against those persons who had robbed them. Cook and his band may have saved themselves from starvation, but their vindictive and deadly activities came to the attention of the Federals who began scouring the middle border from Ozark to the lower North Fork River for them.

In January, of 1865, Lt. Willis Kissee and 25 men on a scouting trip learned of the hideout from an informer. Kissee and his men surrounded the entrance and called out that they would be treated as prisoners of war and not harmed if they surrendered. He gave them four hours to decide. Eleven of the men emerged from the cave, but Cook and two others refused to surrender. Not wishing to risk lives in an effort to take the remaining raiders, Kissee built a huge fire on the ledge above the entrance and pushed it over the cliff into the mouth of the cave where wind blew smoke inside. Blinded and nearly suffocated by the smoke, Cook and his companions emerged from their lair. They were gunned down and left where they fell. The bodies were later retrieved and buried in a common grave overlooking the stream that flowed from the spring at Cook's cave.

A more famous bushwhacker was Alf Bolin, who instituted a reign of terror during the war that is almost unequaled. Bolin, a large, wiry man with a long, chest-length red beard, was a bushwhacker with no allegiance to either North or South. He bragged of having killed more than 40 men, including Calvin Cloud. He was the man, who with his wife, Mary Jane, had taken Bolin in as an orphan and raised him. The masked Bolin shot him in front of Mary Jane, who recognized the voice behind the mask. She was later to play another part in Bolin's life—and death.

Bolin and his band of renegades preyed on defenseless homesteaders, though Bolin was bold enough to bushwhack small units of Union soldiers. The rag-tag band raped, robbed, and murdered persons from Union families over a wide area between Ozark, Missouri, and Crooked Creek, Arkansas, with many of his crimes committed at "Murder Rock," near Kirbyville on the Kirbyville-Harrison Road. So numerous and monstrous were Bolin's crimes that a $5000 reward was offered by the Federal government for his capture, dead or alive, as the Union militia fruitlessly pursued him and his band.

The outlaw's bloody reign was finally ended by Robert Foster and his wife and a 22-year-old corporal from the Iowa Volunteer Cavalry, Zachariah E. Thomas. Thomas was sent to the Foster farm, near Murder Rock, where Bolin had been invited to the cabin by Mrs. Foster on the pretext of having Bolin buy their household goods. On the morning of February 2, 1863, Bolin came to the log cabin. Mrs. Foster told Bolin she was hiding a lone Rebel soldier, the disguised Corp. Thomas. During conversation, Bolin bent down to the fireplace for a coal to light his pipe, and Thomas dealt him a blow to his head with a heavy coulter. He and Mrs. Foster dragged the body outside to a log barn, but Bolin revived as she was cleaning up the blood on the hearthstone in the cabin. Thomas, who was saddling his horse, used the Army Colt that he had never drawn in the cabin to finish off Bolin before leaving. He returned at dawn the next day with 25 Cavalry troops, led by a major and two mule-drawn wagons. Bolin was placed in one wagon and all of the Fosters' meager belongings in the other, and the troop headed toward Forsyth.

In the county seat, news of Bolin's death attracted hundreds of locals who came to view the corpse. When the caravan headed north toward Ozark, a bitter local, Colbert Hays, whose relatives had suffered during Bolin's reign of terror, stopped the procession just north of Forsyth and asked to identify the bushwhacker. He did so, but before the amazed group could stop him, he beheaded the dead Bolin with an ax. The headless body was unceremoniously buried, and with Bolin's bloody head in a gunny sack, the troops continued toward Ozark. At Ozark the head was impaled on a pole and displayed.

It was Mary Jane Cloud, widow of Calvin Cloud and surrogate mother of Alf Bolin, who was ordered to Ozark to make a positive identification of Bolin's head so the reward could be collected.

The guerrilla warfare carried on by the borderland Rebels against the Union forces during the last two years of the war was difficult to "shut off" when surrender was ordered and the war was over. During the war, Ozarks towns had been decimated. Of the 51 structures that comprised Berryville, Arkansas, in 1860, only Hubbert's Hotel and two small residences remained when peace was declared. Yellville, Arkansas was destroyed by Union forces and bushwhackers, and before the fighting ceased 32 buildings had been burned. Dubuque, Arkansas on the White River had been a busy steamboat landing with a thriving community, but the community and landing were totally destroyed by Union forces because the area had a lead smelter that furnished shot for Confederate forces. It was never rebuilt.

In Missouri, six of the counties bordering Arkansas had their county seats destroyed by fire. Rockbridge, the first county seat of Ozark County, was burned and never rebuilt on the old townsite. Vera Cruz, the pre-Civil War county seat of Douglas County, met a similar fate. On April 22, 1863, Union troops burned Forsyth, county seat of Taney County. The county seat towns of Galena in Stone County, and Ozark in Christian County, had incendiary fires but escaped total destruction. The courthouse in Ozark, however, burned soon after hostilities ceased. Farms and homesteads suffered even more, and few remained standing at the end of the war, the inhabitants having fled.

Even the end of the war did not see the end of the factional hatred. Each survivor, each returning refugee, had cause to hate someone. This animosity was nurtured and kept alive in the hearts and minds of many as they began the arduous task of rebuilding homes and lives. It destroyed rational thought. It poisoned the souls of those who were afflicted by it. The lawless period of the war encouraged a general lawlessness, and hatred often flared up in acts of revenge. In the period from 1832 to 1860 only three murders had been reported in Taney County. In the post war period of 1865-1885, there were 40 murders—and not a single conviction.

To combat the lawlessness, vigilance committee organizations were formed in many Ozarks counties. There was the Anti-Horse Thief Association. Another was simply called the Citizens' Committee. Greene County had its "Honest Men's League"—which soon became a part of the problem it attempted to resolve. In Taney County, the "Law-and-Order League" came in existence April 5, 1885 in an outdoor organizational meeting on Snapp Bald. Because its members met on the treeless top of a mountain, known locally as a bald, enemies dubbed the organization "the Bald Knobbers." Its vigilante justice became such a problem the state militia was called out to quell the unrest. Events climaxed with the hanging of three of its members on the Ozark courthouse square, May 10, 1889 but not before the Ozarks had gained national press attention.

The Bald Knobbers were a part of the plot and action of Harold Bell Wright's novel, *The Shepherd of the Hills*, and made this area of the White River watershed famous as a tourist destination in the first half of the 20th century. The Ozarks continues to "promote" its historic past with an outdoor dramatic production of *The Shepherd of the Hills* and "train holdups" by Alf Bolin and his gang at Silver Dollar City, as does Meramec Caverns with its tourist hook of being Jesse James' "hideout."

Half of the actors in the play based on Wright's novel are recent arrivals to the Ozarks and mingle with locals so well you can't tell them apart. The scruffy-looking actor at Silver Dollar City who stops the train filled with tourists and announces, "I'm Alf Bolin and I'm takin' yer valuables," may be a tourist industry worker whose ancestors could have had some actual dealings with the notorious bushwhacker at Murder Rock.

The mock robbery has a happier ending than the victims of the real Alf Bolin. Those 8 million tourists who come to the Ozarks to play golf on the Murder Rock Golf Course or for family fun at Silver Dollar City, or who buy *The Hawksbill Crag* for an interesting read—as well as those of us who live here and may have deep roots here that are long forgotten—should be aware that what now passes for amusement and entertainment has roots in the not-too-distant Ozark past.

—*Fred R. Pfister, editor,* **The Ozarks Mountaineer**

THE HAWKSBILL CRAG

By Richard Oliver Snelson

CHAPTER 1

March 1865
Saint Louis, Missouri

Captain Nelson Paintier limped from the Jefferson Barracks hospital to the barracks corral. When he could stand straight, he topped more than six feet two inches tall. Four years of war battling the Confederate Army had left him gaunt, slightly stooped, and exhausted. His faded blue pants looked out of place with the deer-hide jacket he purchased for the trip home. He knew the pants and any trace of federal service would have to be gone before he reached his home in southern Missouri. Not many there would welcome a former Yankee soldier.

Whipping a lead rope against his good leg, he stopped to look over the herd of horses standing ready for their next call to battle. The day before he had angrily watched the troops drive a hundred or more of the surplus horses to a pit to kill them. His big roan mare had been led to the killing pen this morning. No one was going to stop him from getting her out. He quickened his approach to the corral gate and was confronted by a sentry.

The sentry lifted his rifle in a salute, stepping to his right to block the gate, "You can't go in this pen, mister," the trooper said. "They're killing them horses today."

"Watch me, son," Nelson said, pushing the young trooper aside and stopping with his hand on the gate latch. "Old friend in there, coming out with me."

"You have to stop! Told me nobody goes in there. Sorry, mister."

"Not mister, soldier. Rank's captain to you. Damn it anyway, how old are you, kid?"

"Four . . . four . . . teen. Lied about that," the boy said, staring at the ground.

"Stay at your post, son. I'm going in there after my horse," Nelson said, pushing the gate open and stepping around the guard.

The boy followed close behind Nelson, carrying his rifle at his side.

"Over there, the roan mare that's watching us," Nelson said, giving a short whistle that started the mare pushing her way to his side. "Hello, Blue." Nelson draped his arm over the mare's neck in a hug and slipped his sugar-filled hand under her mouth.

"Bad scar, there on her shoulder," said the trooper.

"Took two minie-balls that day. Both meant for me. I kept her wound open for days so it would drain. Slipped a tube in each morning against her breastbone and blew the wound full of iodine. She stood still, like she knew I was trying to help. One minie's still in there. Mare's got a big heart, son. We fought three battles, leading my troops, after she healed up."

"Scar must be why they had her up for slaughter," said the trooper.

"That, and now they don't need her, with the war being nearly over. Gonna have to look the other way, boy. I'm taking the horse out of here."

"Oh, shit! My lieutenant's heading for the gate," whispered the trooper, again lowering his eyes to the ground.

Nelson tied his lead rope to the horse's halter, scratched the mare behind the ears, and walked to the gate where the officer waited.

"Commander wants you at headquarters," the Lieutenant said, blocking Nelson's way.

"Bullshit," Nelson pushed the lieutenant aside and walked through the gate with the mare. Without looking back he led the horse to where his saddle and tack waited. After he brushed the dirt off the mare's back, Nelson tossed the saddle blanket in place, and carefully worked out the wrinkles. He swung the new saddle on, knowing regret would soon come from having to break in a saddle on a long ride.

"Need you at command, sir. Now! They're holding up your discharge orders," said the flustered lieutenant who had followed closely behind Nelson and the horse.

"Do you see what I'm doing? When I'm done, going to ride the hell out of here and head home. Going back to what's left of southern Missouri. Are you going to try and stop me, Lieutenant?" Nelson firmed up the saddle's girth and tied the end in place.

"No, but he is, sir." The lieutenant pointed toward the commanding general and his aide headed directly for Nelson and his horse.

"Captain Paintier, see you found your old hero war horse my aides told me about. Let's see, you named her Blue?"

"That's right, sir. My enlistment is up and I'm heading back to Steelville, Missouri," Nelson moved to climb in the saddle.

"I wanted to talk with you about something, Captain," the brigadier said, turning to excuse his aides and motioning for Nelson to walk with him. Nelson reluctantly draped the mare's lead rope over a rail and took several quick steps to join the general's side.

"You're from southern Missouri, Captain Paintier. Aware of what's still going on down there?" he asked, not waiting for an answer he continued walking.

"The guerrilla troops who pulled off from Quantrill after he burned down Lawrence, Kansas, are still causing my command trouble. With summer coming on, it will only get worse."

"I've a feeling a lot of those raiders come from around my home town," Nelson said.

"Things got out of hand for me again last week. One of my damn hot-headed officers, named Turner, from the Rolla command caught some of Bloody Bill Anderson's boys south of Jefferson City. Tied them up to trees, spent the rest of the day killing them one by one. Even his troops tried to get him to stop. Last prisoner he whipped until it looked like he had been skinned, tied him on his horse with a note, said more of this is coming," the commander said, as he stopped and turned to face Nelson.

"I know Lieutenant Turner. He's been trouble ever since he got promoted," Nelson said.

"I ordered him arrested and locked him in the stockade at Rolla. I'll hang him myself when I get him back to Saint Louis," the commander said.

"Looks like I might be riding into some hell," Nelson said.

"We had rumors the guerrilla raiders were breaking up before this happened. Jim Hagan and his boys had quit Anderson and went on south to Buffalo River. Turns out the man Turner whipped is Hagan's son. He was half dead when they sent him off on his horse, so I doubt if he lived."

"What's this got to do with me, sir?" Nelson asked.

"Just this, Captain. I don't have any other man who can ride into guerrilla territory and survive. I've got two sets of papers waiting on my desk. One is your discharge. The other an extension of duty and pardons to be signed by Hagan and each of his men. I'll sign the pardons when you bring them back. Take your pick. Up to you which you take. President Lincoln wants the killing to stop in the border states. You can help."

"Fucking almighty generals!" thought Nelson.

* * *

Half a day's ride to the west, Nelson left the well-traveled trace for a backwoods trail that allowed him to travel without attracting attention. Certain his coming home wouldn't stay a secret long, he wanted to delay the news as long as possible. Riding along the ridges and hills of the Ozark Mountains would take a lot longer, but Nelson didn't mind. It gave him time to get clear in his mind why he was really going back to a place where the sheriff had killed his father and tried to do the same to him. Nelson hoped Sheriff Spaid had survived the war; he would be facing Paintier justice soon.

With darkness nearly upon him, Nelson found a place to spend the night under a clump of cedar trees next to a creek. After loosening the saddle's girth, he led Blue to the creek to drink. Back at the cedars he unsaddled and then hobbled the mare to graze a small stand of grass close to the trees. The cold of the March night had started to chill him, so he gathered an armload of fallen branches and lit a small fire. The hardtack biscuits and jerked beef in his saddlebags would have to satisfy his hunger for tonight. With his bedroll spread alongside the fire, he stretched out and leaned against the still-warm leather of his saddle.

Reaching back to his saddlebags, he took out paper and pencil. For more than a year, he had prayed for the chance to go back to the wrongs he needed to fix in Steelville. He put his thoughts on paper about the guilt that stuck with him through battle after battle and always brought back the vision of the slave girl standing on the gallows, her stare burning forever in his mind. He had put off writing this chapter.

Nelson Paintier, 1850
Steelville, Missouri

They came down the path from the dog-trot cabin toward the spring pool, to where I was hiding in the blackberry brambles, waiting. Shivers crossed my back, my pa would beat me till I'm half dead, if he found out I was here, playing with a slave girl. The master's baby girl clung tightly to the edge of the slave girl's sack cloth dress, the baby stumbled now and then, like all babies that were just learning to walk.

It had been months before when I learned the slave girl's owners called her Mary. When she got close, I jumped from behind the bramble. Mary's hand swept to cover her mouth in mock surprise and the baby girl pulled the edge of the sack dress to cover her face. Mary smiled at my prank and then leaned over to kiss the child on the head.

I grabbed Mary's free hand and walked around her, turning her and the baby in a slow circle. When the turning stopped, the baby laughed and pointed toward the water. Mary knelt by the side of the dark flowing spring and reached for the tin ladle hanging on a limb. She filled the ladle with the cold water and held it for the baby girl to drink.

I watched as she leaned over the baby and her sack dress fell open. I must have been staring because Mary frowned at me and quickly closed the front of her dress. It wasn't the first time I saw her nakedness. Months ago I had watched her sitting beside the spring pool, dipping a cloth in the cold water and rubbing it across her breasts, she didn't know I was there hiding behind the bramble bush. I had watched my little sister taking a bath, but seeing the slave girl caused me to feel like a man. I didn't tell anyone what I had seen.

Mary hung the ladle back and then turned away from the spring pool to spread the apron she had been wearing on the ground. After she sat the little girl on the apron, Mary took a small cornhusk doll from the pocket of her dress and put it in the baby's hands. When she straightened, she reached for my hand and turned us dancing to the bubbling of the spring water as it went over the moss covered rock dam. I tugged her arm and backed slowly toward our secret bramble bush hide-away. After a few steps, Mary broke away and went back to check on the baby.

Then she quickly followed me behind the bramble. I dropped to the ground, pulling Mary down beside me. I reached to feel her, to touch her hair. Black as coal, it would spring right back after I pushed it flat on the side of her head. She pushed my hand away, grabbed a hunk of my hair, and yanked hard, laughing and not speaking a word. I reacted, grabbed her around the waist, and rolled over her squirming body. The rolling stopped when we hit the bramble stickers. Mary sat up and carefully picked the bramble stickers from the sackcloth dress, only to rise suddenly and leave to check on the baby at play by the spring. I sat behind the bramble and waited for her to return.

Her screams caused me to jump to my feet and rush around the bramble. She stumbled into me, grabbed my arm, and pulled me toward the place where the apron sat empty.

After staring at the paper for half an hour without writing the next paragraph, Nelson carefully folded the three pages of handwritten memories and wrapped them in the oilskin cover with the pardons he carried for Hagan and his men. The fire's embers still gave off heat so he turned on his side and hoped sleep would finally come.

The next morning Nelson saddled his horse and started again toward southern Missouri and his boyhood home.

Three days of riding had brought him close to Steelville. Nelson could read the roan mare well, her faster pace and alert ears told him a storm would be upon them before the day ended.

A hard pelting rain started around noon and didn't let up.

"Darn coon oil doing no good on this raincoat," he said to the mare. "Feel the wet trickling to the bottom of my drawers."

After three hours of riding in the rain, Nelson dismounted to lead the mare, giving her a much-needed rest.

"Come on old gal, know you would like to stop for a while," Nelson said, urging the horse to follow him up a steep rock trail. At the top, he stopped and pulled the slack out of the saddle's girth, the trail had gotten too slick for him to walk, so he climbed back in the saddle. "You can handle it better than I can, horse."

Heading down the far side of the hill, he leaned back in the saddle pushing his feet forward in the stirrups, balancing against the steep descent and the sliding horse. Nelson felt like he was on a runaway train when all four of the mare's feet broke loose. Blue locked her front legs and struggled with her hindquarters to keep her balance and stop the slide. Nelson cleared his feet from the stirrups to keep from being pinned if the mare fell. The slide slowed as the mare gained footing in the rear and ended with them wedged safely against a cedar tree. He leaned over the mare's neck and patted her, a thank you, for again saving his neck. With no place for shelter, he rode on into the night.

The rain continued throughout the night, with the sound of thunder only a heartbeat behind the blinding lightning strikes that seemed to follow Nelson and the mare.

He thought by morning when he reached the Meramec River he could swim the mare across, but the rain didn't stop and now he was sure he would have to wait for the river to fall before crossing. The ridge he followed would take him alongside the stream in a few hours.

The wind had picked up and changed directions several times in the last few minutes. Frequent lightning strikes with thunderclaps rattled his teeth and rolled through the valley. The horse slowed with its ears turned toward the deep Meramec valley Nelson had been paralleling.

"What's wrong, gal?" Nelson asked, standing in the saddle to listen. "Now, I hear it too. Sounds like half the trees in the valley are being yanked up."

He nudged Blue down a trail leading to the river's edge. As they neared the bottom of the hill, the trail ended at a small clearing right at the Meramec River's swollen edge.

He dropped the reins onto the mare's neck. "Easy, Blue. Whoa, gal!"

The dim morning's light caused Nelson's tired eyes and mind to play tricks on him. He saw strange shapes that swam in the foaming water, huge monsters that rolled and dived, playing in the currents that blocked his path.

In his mind, he heard the monsters scream as they twisted in the tumbling waters. Screams like others he tried to forget. Screams mixed with blood that gushed from wounded men's mouths. Men left on the battlefield by a Union general too stubborn and proud to ask for two hours of ceasefire to collect his wounded troops.

Nelson pulled his raincoat hood tight against his ears and started to dismount to wait out the flood.

"Help! Somebody . . . please! We need help! Please . . . God!"

The woman's screams and cries for help came from what looked like a floating roof, twisting in the river current. Nelson jerked the hood off his head, grabbed the reins, and stood in the stirrups. Blue reared, pawing the air, it was another call to battle for the mare.

9

A tree on the hillside behind them exploded as lightning struck. Stinging pieces hit like fragments from a cannon blast. Nelson didn't hear the bugle sound the charge, but Blue did, he felt the mare clench the bit in her teeth and then plunge far out into the raging river.

The current dragged him from the saddle and swept him into a dark pool of suffocation. He thrashed his way to the top, reaching to find the saddle and Blue. Too far away. The mare's eyes were wide, her nostrils flared. He saw her look toward the rider she trusted. He couldn't help her. Blue was caught in a whirlpool that drew her down.

Nelson struggled to keep his nose above the rolling sea of mud and water. He caught glimpses of the openings between half-submerged trees as the river swept him downstream. The current was too fast. More screams for help came as Nelson hit the side of the roof turning in the currents. The screams stopped, and a woman clutched at his arm helping him climb onto the roof.

"Help us," the woman pleaded, "Water came up so fast. We climbed out the attic onto the roof."

Nelson shook his head, coughed out the water, and looked around the tiny island that had saved him. His blurry eyes followed the woman's arm and pointing finger.

"My boy!" The woman crawled frantically across the roof toward the boy.

"Please . . . Please, mister. Save him!" she cried.

The roof smashed into a boulder on the river's bottom and threw Nelson to the edge once again. Still, he struggled toward the woman and boy. The woman reached out, over the edge of the roof trying to grab her son's arm.

A fallen tree lodged across the roof's path swept across Nelson's back and caught the mother's legs in its tangled grip. Nelson grabbed for her arm and missed. She hung there in the tree limbs for seconds then vanished beneath the dark water behind the spinning roof. There were no screams or cries for help.

"Hang on boy. I'll get you." Nelson rolled across the roof to the boy and reached for his hand.

"Take my hand and pull hard," Nelson said.

In one quick pull, Nelson had the boy beside him on the roof. Only the sound of the water churning in whirlpools came from behind them.

"I can't see her," the boy stood and looked behind the floating roof.

"I know, boy. The tree . . . the river . . . Keep hanging on."

Nelson heard the crack of boards breaking away from beneath the roof. It sank still deeper into the brown current.

"Where did she go?" the boy asked, wiping his eyes.

"You've got to be brave, boy. Got to help when it's time to jump and swim for the bank."

The roof tilted. Nelson shifted his weight to keep it from tipping over. He knew somewhere ahead the stream widened and the current would slow. It would give him a chance to save the boy. They would wait.

The rotations of the spinning roof became a count for Nelson of the years since he had left this valley. The count reached fifteen before he stopped. He had run away then, fifteen years old, and swore to return. He knew he would come back for unfinished business someday. The current slowed; they were rounding a bend.

"Get ready boy. When we get closer to the bank we're going to jump into the willow trees."

The boy still stared back up the river. Nelson grabbed his arms and lifted him to his feet as the roof brushed the submerged willow tops along the flooded bank.

"Now! Jump!"

Nelson shoved him with all the energy he had left. The boy splashed into the willow tops, then sank. Nelson dove after him, touched the boy's head first, and then gripped his waist, to lift him to the surface. With the boy's weight holding him underwater, Nelson's feet bounced on the willow limbs as the current pushed him over them. Nelson did a strange dance that kept the boy's head from going under the water. Nelson's breath was gone, and he almost forgot the precious cargo the mother had begged him to save. He kicked to the surface for air. The boy was still there in front of him. His arms went tight around the boy again. Nelson saw white bark, the top of a sycamore tree sticking out of the water.

"Grab the limbs. Grab now!"

They hit the limb together, both getting arms around the white bark. Nelson's feet bounced on top of the water under the limb; the boy climbed up and then reached to help him. Nelson hung over the limb like wet laundry in the wind.

"Climb higher, boy, the water's still coming up."

"I ain't no boy. Name is Joshua."

CHAPTER 2

"Stay awake, Joshua," Nelson said. "I feel like an old coon up here in this sycamore, treed by a pack of hounds." He tried to get the boy to talk during the night, keep him awake, so he wouldn't lose his grip and fall into the water. The boy never answered. Sometime in the night the rising water reached Nelson's knees, and then it started to fall. The river crest passed, and morning found them both safe.

Nelson shook the boy. "You still awake?"

"I was supposed to keep my Mom safe."

"This river gets wild when it's flooded. Sucked my horse right out from under me," Nelson moved to get a better grip on the limb.

"Mister, can you find my mom?"

"We can look for her on the way back to Steelville. I need to get you back home."

"I don't want to go . . . back there," he said.

"It's your home. The town, Steelville, is your home, isn't it?"

"It's gone. Our home is gone," Joshua said.

"Your dad, won't he be looking for you?"

"No, he won't. He don't stay there no more. Went off to guerrilla fight."

"How long since he's been home?" Nelson asked.

"Only time he comes home is when the leaves are thick on the trees," Joshua said.

Nelson understood what the boy said. The guerrilla raiders needed the thick tree cover for safety and would head south for Arkansas and Texas when fall and winter came.

In the cloudy afternoon light Nelson saw the fields along the river were full of huge brush piles and heaps of trash washed in by the flash flood.

"River's gone down a lot. We can try for the bank now," Nelson said, sliding down the slick trunk into the knee-deep water.

Joshua followed, but his arms were too short to grip the big tree trunk. He slipped, splashing face down into the muddy water. His head popped up wearing a sheepish look and dripping mud.

"At least I ain't thirsty no more," Joshua said.

Nelson chuckled for the first time since he had taken the mare from the killer pens in Saint Louis.

Being barefoot didn't keep Joshua from straying to search around each pile of brush and lumber. "Try to stay up with me, Joshua. The mud is only ankle deep," Nelson said, realizing for the first time he still had his boots on and the boy was barefooted.

"Hey, mister. Look here, sticking out of the boards."

When Nelson saw the legs of a rust-colored cow stuck straight out in death, he thought of their milk cow. The pool of water below the dead cow's udder had turned white from the milk dripping from her teats.

When he was a boy their cow would stand at the barn-yard gate, with a drooping udder and leaking teats, bellowing for him to come milk. When his dad found out he had been off trapping or hunting and neglecting the cow a butt whipping always came after he finished the milking.

He reached and stripped the milk from one of the extended teats of the dead cow, thinking of something to drink.

"You're crazy, Mister. I ain't goin' t' drink no milk from a dead cow."

"One time during the war, we were so hungry, would have pulled that cow out of the brush pile and butchered it for supper."

"I'm glad we ain't hungry yet," Joshua said.

The fields were littered with belongings from the town, wooden buckets, a door to an outhouse, wagon parts, harness, tables and broken chairs all sticking from the huge piles of trees. Nelson stooped to open a leather bound book lying half submerged in the mud and water and saw land grants and plots that marked-out the town's homesteads. He wondered if all the courthouse records were gone. Looking up, his eyes fixed on a hand partially covered with mud and branches.

"Stay here, Joshua."

Mud splashed on his side as the boy rushed past, ignoring Paintier's command. He watched Joshua claw at the brush and tree limbs, shoving and pushing them away from the hand and arm.

"It's not her, Joshua. Look! Look here, see, it's a man."

The boy stopped tearing at the pile and stood stooped over staring at the dead man's hand and the small metal object sticking between his fingers. Nelson's fingers slipped off the object as he tried to pull it from the hand's death grip. He pried the thumb up and took the dirty object to swirl it in the pool of muddy water around his boots.

"What is it?" Joshua asked.

"A toy soldier, someone that led the south in battle," Nelson replied.

"Is it General Robert E. Lee," Joshua asked.

"Yes, would you like to keep the toy?"

"It's not a toy, mister," Joshua stated, "We all have them hid somewhere. They made them secret at the ironworks out of Yankee gunmetal. Then we gave them to the rebs to make bullets."

"Here, keep it, Joshua. Lee is a fine soldier and general. Better than most of the ones the Yankees have."

Nelson and the boy cleared the rest of the brush from the man's body. The man had only one arm, his other missing from a shoulder that showed signs of recent healing. Joshua said he remembered the man from Steelville and how he told them he lost the arm at the Wilson's Creek Battle.

"Remember where we found the man, Joshua, so we can tell the searchers where to find him," Nelson said.

The river valley narrowed and they were forced to climb up along the bluffs that lined the north side of the Meramec River. Nelson knew the trail there lead to the Meramec Iron Works and the worker's cabin village they called Stringtown. The Stringtown cabins were above the river and wouldn't be flooded; so they could get food and supplies there.

When Nelson reached the top of the bluff he saw smoke rising from a cooking fire close to a mile away. He led the boy across a narrow cut in the bluff and climbed the steep trail leading toward the smoke. In the evening twilight, Nelson could make out the figures of two men sitting up close to a small fire. He heard the uneasy braying of mules warning someone was approaching. The men dropped to the ground and two shots rang out.

"Hold on damn it," Nelson yelled.

"Who are you mister?"

"Can me and the boy come on in?"

"Send the boy in first, then you can follow. Get them hands up over your head so we can see them."

A sideboard wagon sat behind the men with a high-line tie between two trees that extended over eight mules. The two mules on the end paced and snorted with their tall ears pointing at the approaching strangers. Nelson knew the alert mules were the lead team of the hitch. He walked into camp with his hands over his head. He could smell roasting meat and heard the boiling of a fresh pot of coffee on the fire. Joshua hadn't looked up since he saw the skewered squirrels.

"By the looks of your muddy clothes both you'ns need some warmin' up and somethin' to eat," said the gray bearded man, "Squirrel 'bout done."

"The boy and I were caught in the flood last night. His home got washed away," Nelson said.

"We watched this morning. Looked like the whole of Steelville was coming out of the draw and heading down river."

"Boy and me, we spent the night on a sycamore limb. Name's Nelson, boy is Joshua."

"Me and him, Gales and Lomax. We haul the iron bars and slag iron blooms up to Hermann, where they put 'em on Missouri River steamboats headed for Saint Louis. Four mule teams hitched up to two tons of iron aboard. We're headed back to the ironworks. We got to watch who comes around these days. They had us start carrying the Sharps carbines after the bushwhackers hit the company store 'bout two months ago."

"Are the bushwhackers raiding much in these parts?" Nelson asked.

"They ride through town, worse than the damn union cavalry," said Lomax. "At least we knew what to expect from the Yankees. With the bushwhackers, they hit their own kind of folks, rob and steal and do worse with the women folk. They take everything that ain't nailed down. Ain't safe, don't matter where you go."

"Wonder if we could hitch a ride tomorrow? I want to get the boy back into Steelville; they'll be looking for him for sure."

"Yep. For now, you two pull off a hunk of one of them squirrels. Bet you ain't 'et all day," said Lomax. "One of us is going to be up all night keeping watch on them mules. So eat and curl up by the fire. We're keeping her blazing all night."

The roasted squirrel legs reminded Nelson of meals when he was a boy. He brought home a lot of squirrels for his mother to cook. It was easy to sit under a hickory nut tree and ambush a dozen in one morning, a game he liked to play.

It came back to mind, like it had for years, the ambush, that had burned his house and killed his dad. He knew who was responsible and wanted to face them. He wondered if

Steelville had forgotten the fifteen-year-old boy that disappeared the day they hanged the slave girl, Mary.

"Thanks for helping me mister," Joshua said. "It ain't your fault she's gone. It's mine. I promised my aunt I would take care of my mother."

"It's nobody's fault, Joshua. Some things, we just don't know why they happen. Try and get some sleep now."

The boy turned away, resting his head on a fallen limb and said no more. Nelson scooted lower against the oak and was soon asleep.

Joshua shook Nelson awake while it was still dark to tell him the men had the teams hitched ready to go.

"Come on, mister. They're waiting for us," Joshua said.

"Name's Nelson, Joshua, Nelson Paintier. I'm coming, get on that wagon, we're headed for Stringtown."

The team driver pushed the eight mules along the narrow trails at a pace Nelson thought was insane. One hour into the trip, Nelson saw the four riders first. They came up fast from behind. Nelson thought there wasn't much to steal from an empty wagon, maybe they were after the new rifles the drivers carried?

"Lomax, got some riders on our tail," he said.

"Just saw them, goddam bushwhackers," said Lomax. "Know how to shoot one of these?"

"Damn right I do," Nelson said, grabbing the carbine Lomax offered him, before pushing Joshua to the floor of the wagon.

The riders started firing first, over the flattened ears of their four horses. The feel of the kill was still fresh in Nelson's mind—his saber drawn, splitting a skull, cutting a throat, or cleaving an arm. The rifle was cleaner. He didn't have to look close at what he killed. His first shot pitched the lead rider backward in a somersault over the back of the horse. The three remaining riders were soon joined by four others who seemed to come out of nowhere. Lomax took a shot to the back of his neck and fell forward to the floor of the wagon. A surge of blood stained the wagon's floor.

"Gales, what the hell you fellows packing that those fellows want so damn bad?"

"It's under the seat in the saddlebags. Iron Work's payroll. We picked it up from the steamboat."

"They're going to kill us if they get us stopped, Gales," Nelson said. "Throw the saddlebags on the road. They'll stop for that."

"Can't do that, mister. Lose my job," said Gales.

"Rather lose your life? If they don't shoot you, I'm going to, if you don't throw that payroll off this wagon," Nelson said.

"Throw it, goddam it; throw it," said Gales.

Nelson jerked the saddlebag covers open and tossed the money into the air behind the wagon. The coins and bills hit the road in clouds of red dust behind the wagon. The riders pulled up, jumped off their horses, and dove for the floating bills.

"I think that'll keep them busy for quite a while," Nelson said. "Give us time to get to Stringtown." He thought again of his lost saddlebags and pardons; he would have to find them before anyone else did.

CHAPTER 3

In a second floor office of the Missouri Capitol Building in Jefferson City, a senator stood at the window with his binoculars, watching the side-wheel ferryboat angle against the current and ease into Loman's landing. The steamboat was filled with passengers from Callaway County and points north and east.

"Is your man on the ferry, judge?" the seated man asked, as he propped his feet on the senator's desk.

"It's "Senator" to you. Get your fucking feet off my desk, Spaid. I haven't been a judge since we left Steelville before the war. Remember, Sheriff Spaid?"

"It's just Spaid now, your highness," He dropped his boots to the floor.

"He comes every two weeks. Brings me the news of what the high muckety muck army officers are up to in Saint Louis," said the senator. "Last I heard they were going after Bloody Bill Anderson and his boys, even if they had to chase them clear into Texas. Relax, have a drink, Spaid. I see him climbing the steps from the landing now." *Oh, yes, Spaid's always trying to follow in my footsteps. So many mistakes in his shaded history. Be gone, Spaid. Be gone.*

"Come in, George. You're out of breath. Lots of steps to climb, coming up from the river's bank. Come in and have a seat," the senator said.

"Thank you, sir." George dropped into a chair next to the senator's desk.

"Meet my friend from our Steelville days, Sheriff John Spaid."

"Just Spaid, George," he said.

"How are things at Gratiot Street Prison? How many Confederates left in there?" The senator turned to look out the window again.

"Thinned down some. Yankees pardon them and send them packing with little more than the worn-out clothes on their backs and no shoes on their feet. Leave it to the Yankees to try and strip the very hearts out of their prisoners," said George, turning to look at Spaid.

"It's okay, George. Spaid hates the nigger-loving Yankees as much as we do," whispered the senator, still looking at the river. "Have to keep that quiet these days. They have spies and informers all through this building."

"I should keep my hatred for the Yankees out of this," George said.

"Hagan's been raiding down south again. What troops are they sending against him?" the senator asked.

"They sent one man, undercover, to try and get in with Hagan and his men. Orders are to either capture or pardon him. Pressure is high from Washington to have the guerilla fighters lay down their weapons and go home," said George. "Stop the raiding and killing."

"One man? The guerrillas will have him strung up in less than a week. Know who he is, George?"

"Name's Paintier. Captain Nelson Paintier. He fought for the North, but comes from Hagan's stomping grounds."

The senator turned quickly from the window, "Paintier?"

"Yes, sir, Captain Paintier. He fought the war leading nigger troops back east. Command called him a hero. Some say he's writing a book about his life when he was a boy in Steelville, when you hanged that slave girl."

"Thank you, George." The senator took an envelope filled with cash from his desk drawer, and handed it to the informant.

"See you next trip, George," the senator said, hurrying him out the office door.

"You sure were in a hurry to get George gone," said Spaid.

"Find him, Spaid. Find that damn Paintier and be sure you kill the nigger-loving little bastard this time."

"Who?"

"Paintier, you idiot. The same Paintier I told you to kill along with that headstrong old man of his. Made hell for me, after I sentenced that murdering slave girl to hang. Even came up here to the capitol, trying to get help for her. Claimed the slave girl didn't drown the baby. You let him get away, Spaid!"

"He's a dead man, Judge," said Spaid, picking up his hat.

"He better be, Spaid. A book of his would ruin my chances to be governor of this state."

CHAPTER 4

Gales pulled the hitch of mules to a stop on the bluff above the ironworks. "Is this where you and the boy wanted to get left?"

"This will do fine. Let me help you with Lomax," Nelson said.

The two men covered the body with one of the wagon tarpaulins.

"Where will you take him, mister?" Joshua asked.

"The company men will just bring him back up here to this cemetery and bury him today," Gales said, "Glad you two was with us. Drove off those damn killers back there."

"Didn't expect a fight on the way here," Nelson said, "Thanks anyway for the ride."

Nelson walked to the bluff edge and stopped beside a weathered white stone. He remembered back when he had been a proud ten-year-old boy arriving at the ironworks with his family from their Virginia home.

He had stood behind his mother and little sister Caroline on his father's going-west wagon as the oxen strained hard into the yoke, climbing the Stringtown Road that wound along a narrow ridge lined with shanties and cabins.

Caroline leaned on her mother's shoulder singing, like she always did when she was happy. The people along the road listened, to her clear voice singing *"All in the merry month of May, When green buds they were swellin'"* His dad walked beside the oxen, urging them to pull harder. Nelson and his sister had named them Bert and Oren. People all along the Stringtown road were out of their cabins watching the newcomers to the ironworks.

"Where are we going to live?" Nelson asked.

"Your dad said it was near the top of the hill," his Ma answered.

"Can we walk now, Pa?" Nelson yelled.

"Stay in the wagon. We got a team and a big wagon loaded with ore coming down the hill. It's going to be hard to pass. We got to get way over to the side."

Nelson saw the wagon and the large hitch of oxen coming down the road. The driver had hurried to the lead team and gotten in front to try to stop his lumbering load.

"Get that yoke and wagon off the road," shouted the team driver. "We're carrying a ton of ore. Oxen can't hold her back!"

Nelson felt the panic in his father's voice as he shouted and hit both oxen hard on the back with the stick. "Gee, ox! Gee over!"

Bert and Oren obeyed his commands, moving far over and knocking down the rails of a yard fence. The oxen were jolted to a stop, hard against the yoke when the front wheel of the wagon jammed against a gate post.

"Ginny, get the kids out. Get away from the wagon," yelled Nelson's father. The ore wagon frame squealed against the wheels as the tongue twisted from the teams not moving together. Nelson heard the crack when the tongue snapped in two. The wagon rolled free and flipped over on its side, skidded past a cabin, smashed into a boulder and catapulted into the air, end over end, down the hill toward them. Nelson jumped from the top of the seat and landed hard on his knees on the rock-strewn yard of the cabin. He looked back to see his mother helping Caroline down over the tall wagon wheel. He wanted her to hurry. At the bottom Caroline caught her foot between the wheel and the rail fence. The thud of the ore wagon impacting the road stung

Nelson's feet; the wagon spewed a red cloud of dust and black hunks of ore into the air. His mother froze, staring up the hill at the wreck coming down on them.

Their oxen broke the yoke and stampeded between the shacks when the lunging wagon and hail of iron ore and dust smashed into the place where his sister had fallen. The red blanket of dust was too thick; he couldn't see her. Nelson crawled toward the place he saw her fall. His father was there trying to lift the broken wheel lying across Caroline's chest.

Nelson heard the sucking, wheezing sound that dying cattle make when butchered, except the sound came from his sister Caroline's crushed throat.

Her eyes looked past the man at her side. They asked for her brother's help. Her fingers extended and reached for brother's hand. He reached to grab them, but they fell limply to the ground. He heard his mother cry out, "Caroline!"

The women of Stringtown carefully lifted the wheel from his sister and carried her to the front of one of the cabins. His dad followed, but stopped to kneel by his wife's side and looked up when a black girl started to brush the dirt from Caroline's face.

"Get away from her," he shouted.

It was the next day when the workers placed Caroline in a small wooden coffin and buried her in the Stringtown Cemetery. After everyone else had left, Nelson stood beside her grave and looked out across the valley. He noticed the turquoise blue water that flowed from the big spring and thought how much she would have liked to sit there smelling the wild blooming lilacs and feeling the wind whip up the valley on its way to lift the hawks soaring above.

Nelson looked again at the turquoise blue water from the spring and then at Joshua, stooped in front of the white stone.

"Caroline Paintier," Joshua read. "Did you know her?"

"She was my sister."

"All of those little stones in rows across the cemetery, they're so close together," said Joshua.

"They're children buried there, Joshua. Most only a few months old. Killed by cholera, whooping cough, consumption, lots of other sicknesses."

"Lucky to have any kids left to grow up," said Joshua.

"Only the strong ones made it, back then in Stringtown."

"You survived, Nelson. Must mean you're strong," said Joshua.

"Could mean lots of other things too. Maybe it's because I was weak and left here."

"Naw, not you, Nelson. My ma wasn't strong. Do you think she survived?"

"I don't know. The flood . . . the current . . .we should pray your mother is safe with God," Nelson said.

"I want to look for her. Like the man we saw in the brush pile, the searchers need to know where she is."

"I'll help you look for her once we get something to eat and a horse," he said.

The years and the war had changed Stringtown. Only the cemetery had grown. The lean-to huts the slaves had lived in were crumbled into history, and most of the cabins he remembered were gone. Nelson walked to touch a stone fireplace standing in the middle of a bed of charcoal, the remains of the home of someone he once knew. He noticed only a small number of people were still living there to work the forges.

They passed the spot on the road, the spot where Caroline's dark red blood met the bright red clay of Stringtown Road. Nelson's eyes were damp. He could still see her reaching, reaching for his hand. He didn't tell Joshua about that day, at least not yet.

"Joshua, go just over yonder and take a look at the ironworks. I've got to get us some grub and a horse."

The boy walked away, his head down, kicking rocks with his toes. Nelson headed over the small ridge toward the company store.

"Howdy, mister," said a broad-shouldered man who rubbed the side of his face with his leather apron to wipe off the black soot.

"Blacksmith?" Nelson asked.

"Yep. What brings you to the ironworks?" he asked.

"Looking for a horse and grub."

"I can take care of getting you something to ride," he said. "See me after you've 'et. Union army took most of the horses from this part of the country. Them the Army didn't get, the bushwhackers took. Reckon a mule be okay 'stead of a horse?"

"Sure rather have a horse. Mule good and broke?"

"Sure, mister. It's about as broke as a mule ever gets."

Nelson smiled and let that one go.

He headed for the company store. He had a money belt of Yankee dollars but didn't want to draw attention to where he was from. He took out a couple of gold pieces he'd been carrying before going in.

"Welcome to the Meramec Iron Works, fella," said the clerk. "What goods you looking for?"

"Got caught in the flood; lost my horse and most else. Boy with me is from Steelville. Taking him back there cause he lost his mother in the river."

"What's the boy's name?" he asked.

"Name's Joshua. Lived with his mother. Dad must have left for the war."

"Would that be Joshua Spencer? Some say his dad is traveling with the bushwhackers; name is Dyer Spencer. Took off right after the war started, came home, found his wife had been bedding down with some Yankee officer guarding the ironworks."

"Boy said his dad left," Nelson replied.

"'Spect he did. Right after Spencer left, the officer and three escort troopers were shot on the road between here and Rolla. Some say the escort troops had just burned out the Biggs and raped their daughter. May have needed killing, some say. Boy's got an aunt, teaches school in Steelville. He stayed with her a lot when his mother was out drinking and such. What you be needin' to get outfitted?"

"Lost my sidearm and rifle in the water, so show me one of those new Sharps carbines and that Griswold .44 should do just fine in my holster. I'll need a skillet, a pan and some food for me and the boy. Reckon that mule the blacksmith is trying to sell me will come with a saddle and some saddlebags, so I'll ride him over to load up."

"That mule! You might be a tad better off and get here quicker if you lead him. Sure know your firearms though, mister. Where did you say you fought?" the storekeeper asked.

Nelson started toward the blacksmith's barn. "I didn't say."

The storekeeper was right. The mule made several rebellious circles around the blacksmith's shop and the mule pen. It wasn't going anywhere without persuasion. When persuasion didn't work, Nelson led him to the store.

CHAPTER 5

.The mule's bred-in-stubbornness took hold even more when Nelson and the boy started for Steelville. With both of them on the mule's back, the animal went in circles always turning back to the stable where its long time mule buddy was braying. Jerking on the reins and pounding on the mule's sides with his boots did little to move it along any quicker. Nelson realized he would have to walk and lead the stubborn mule away from the blacksmith's shop.

About a mile from the ironworks, Nelson stopped and tied the mule up to a fence in front of an old cabin.

"Got him far enough away from his mule buddy, we should be able to ride from here on," Nelson said.

"Do you know who lived here, Nelson?" Joshua asked.

It had been years since Nelson helped carry the flat stones for the foundation and stacked the heavy logs to build the walls of the cabin. The hard work kept the thoughts of how his sister died away, for a while.

"Joshua, I want you to stay here for a couple of minutes and watch that gosh-dang excuse for a mule."

Nelson left the boy and headed down a worn path behind the cabin to an old running spring. He stopped at the edge of the round pool's mirror surface and closed his eyes. The memory of what he had seen there, the baby's face with eyes open, staring at him from below the water's surface — would it still be there when he looked? Nelson turned without looking and headed back up the trail to the cabin and the boy.

"Whose cabin is this?" Joshua asked.

"Don't know who owns it now, Joshua. My dad and I built it. Sold it to the Mockbees a few years later when my mother died."

"Mockbee? I've heard that name before. Is this where they lived?" Joshua asked.

"Yes. Some of their children are buried there in the little cemetery with the headstones. Don't have time now; we need to get on down the ridge if we're going to make Steelville by dark," he said.

"Will we have light enough to look for my mom?" Joshua asked.

"I don't think we will today, Joshua."

Nelson and the boy stopped on the hilltop overlooking the town of Steelville. Nelson had planned to take the boy and search some of the river bottoms when they reached Steelville, but fooling with the contrary mule had made it too late for that.

Much of the town along the creeks had been washed away, leaving only stone foundations and the shell of a former courthouse.

Years ago on the day before the slave girl was hanged he had climbed a wall to sit outside her cell behind the courthouse. He could still remember the exact words Mary had spoken from the window.

"They done tole me tomorrow be the last time I see the morning. What do I believe, with all they done tole me this last cold freezin' winter and all the hot burnin' summer? Done tole me they's goin' to save me. Ain't gonna let them hang no slave child. No sir, white lawyer man's gonna save me. Save me, so jail men can bend me over again and poke me. Then they gonna laugh and beat me till the shit done come right out me."

Stumbling from disgust, Nelson ran home. The next morning all Steelville and Crawford County stood proud outside the courthouse, as everyone watched the trapdoor drop and the rope snap tight around the fourteen-year-old girl's neck.

Nelson looked at the southwest corner, of what remained of the courthouse, the exact spot he had watched her die. Now there was only bare scrubbed ground.

Across from them, on a rise above Yadkin Creek, the bell tower of a church pealed out. The church doors were open for the people of Steelville's vigil. A wagon pulled up in front of the church. A man ran to the sideboards, lifted a blanket, and fell to his knees, hiding his face. The survivors were mourning the town's dead.

"Over by where the road crosses the creek was a bridge. We lived close by the bridge," Joshua said.

"Where is your aunt's house, Joshua? Is it still here?"

"Up by the schoolhouse on the hill. That's where she teaches."

"Let's cross to the church and try and find her. She must be terrible worried about you," Nelson said.

Joshua led the way down the steep hill and across the creek. The crowd on the church steps got larger, all staring, trying to identify the man and boy leading a mule up the hill toward them.

Nelson saw a woman take an uncertain step forward and then another. She covered her mouth with her hands and ran toward the boy. "Oh, my God! Oh, my God! Is that you, Joshua?" she cried out as she ran. "I thought you were dead."

Joshua didn't answer; he stopped with arms at his side and head down. The woman knelt to grab him in her arms. Nelson noticed the beauty of the woman's smile and the radiance caused by the shining tears that crossed her cheeks.

"Say something, Joshua. Say something," she said.

"I'm sorry. I let her drown," Joshua said.

"Who? Joshua. You didn't let her drown."

"My ma, I think she drowned . . . in the river. I was supposed to look after her."

"Joshua, there was nothing anyone could do. The water came up so fast, so many people are missing," she said, "It's no one's fault. God's will is not always understood."

"I'm sorry to interrupt at a time like this, but there was nothing anybody could do to save her. It's not your fault she's gone, Joshua," Nelson said.

"Look here at my face, Joshua. We can thank God you are safe, here with me." She looked up, "Where did you find him, mister?"

"He found us on the river, rode his horse in, trying to save me and my mom," said Joshua. "His name is Nelson."

"Last name is Paintier, ma'am."

"Thank you, Mr. Paintier. I don't know what I would have done if I had lost this boy. He means more than life to me. Joshua's mother is my sister. I'm Ruth Anne Gordon."

"Pleasure, ma'am. Wish it was under better circumstances."

"Joshua, come with me. We must go to the church now. Mr. Paintier, is your name spelled P-A-I-N-T-I-E-R?"

"Why, yes ma'am, it is. Do you know the name?"

"I can't remember where. Anyway, please come to my house later. I'll fix supper for both you and Joshua," she said.

"I need to find a place to tie the mule, and get cleaned up, then I'll be there."

"Most of the town is gone, but I have an empty barn up the ridge by my house," she said, "I won't mind if you use it. I'll send Joshua for you when supper's ready."

"Thanks, Mrs. Gordon."

"Miss." She glanced back over her shoulder as they walked up the hill toward the church, her arm clutching Joshua again and again to her side.

After leading the mule up the hill and tying it in the barn, Nelson returned to the church. He wanted to look for his father's grave in the church cemetery. When he passed the church window, Nelson could see Joshua sitting on the floor, his chin on his knees, alongside a blanket-covered corpse. He watched Ruth Anne kneel beside the boy and push his hair back from his eyes.

The lamplight that came through the church windows created a walkway Nelson followed through the granite and limestone markers of the graveyard that crowded against the church on the steep hillside.

He stopped in front of a narrow white stone and ran his finger across a boy child's name, he didn't recognize, and then still along the 1Yr 6M 22D, spelling out another short life of the times past. His hand brushed the top of each stone as he walked on, searching.

Nelson knelt at the foot of the grave and bowed his head. The lamplight from the church window lit the tombstone's face and caused dark shadows in the deeply carved letters. He looked up to see Miss Gordon standing with the tombstone between them.

"I didn't mean to startle you, Mr. Paintier," she said.

"A bit, Miss Gordon."

"Is this a relative of yours?"

"My father's grave. He was murdered the day before I left Steelville. I wasn't sure where they buried him."

"I'm sorry, Mr. Paintier. You've been gone from here a long time?"

"More that fifteen years."

"Are you here for a while? I'm sorry, that was rude and not any of my business."

"I thought a lot about coming back to this valley all during the war. I plan to stay. My home will always be here."

"They found my sister's body, Mr. Paintier, Joshua is in the church beside her. I'm going to gather him up, and if you could meet us at my house up past the school, I'll feed you both."

"Thank you, ma'am. I'm sorry you lost your sister."

Nelson waited at the bottom of the church steps for the woman and boy to return. Seeing the stone on his dad's grave had reminded him of the ambush that waited for them when they returned home from watching the drunken crowd that had been milling around the courthouse, shouting to lynch the slave girl. It was the night before he fled north.

Ruth Anne came down the church steps, "Joshua must have gone ahead."

"Do you mind if we walk together?" Nelson asked.

"If you don't mind a few questions as we go?"

"Like why I left Steelville?"

"Well, maybe not quite so bluntly," she said, "but yes."

"They burned our house and killed my father. They were trying to kill me too," he said. "I have some of the answers to what happened; only have to put them together."

"You waited a long time to come back, Mr. Paintier. Why so long?"

"I thought for a while I would never come back, but the war changed that."

Nelson thought of the one charge over the wounded Negro bodies who had fought ahead of him. In his mind he could still feel the Negro sergeant drag him away from the swarm of butternut Confederate troops, hell bent on sticking a bayonet through the black troop's white commanding officer. The man's actions had sealed his conviction to return for the slave girl.

The stoop of Ruth Anne's house sat bare. The windows were dark. She went to the door and called out for the boy, but no answer. Nelson thought maybe Joshua might have wanted to sit in the dark alone, after all he had been through. "I'll get a lantern, Mr. Paintier. He may have gone up to the barn to check on the mule."

Nelson saw the flicker of a match through the window and then the glow of the coal-oil lantern that framed her outline. He breathed in the picture of her standing there. Her youth and beauty had made a strong impression on his lonely heart. She returned with the lantern and turned up the hill to the barn.

"He's not in the house. I wonder why he didn't wait for me at the church?" she said.

"I talked to him some on the river. He kept telling me he was responsible for losing his mother from the roof. I think he was ashamed to see you, Miss Gordon."

Nelson admired the glow of the woman's black hair as she held the lantern above her head to light the way through the barn. He tried not to stare when he realized he was alone in an empty barn with a beautiful woman.

"Mule's gone. I left him tied in the stall. It kept wanting to head back to his team mate at the ironworks."

"Could he have gotten loose?" she asked.

"Don't think so," Nelson said.

He reached for the handle of the lantern, her fingers were soft and warm against his. Her fingers lingered before releasing the lantern.

"I put the saddle here on the stall divider. It's gone too."

"We have to stop him, Mr. Paintier. He's gone looking for his dad. Dyers is riding with Confederate guerrilla fighters turned bushwhackers. They still rob and kill without reason," she said.

"As soon as it's light we can get a search party to look for him," Nelson suggested.

"A search party wouldn't stand a chance of finding him. The bushwhackers are like a pack of ghosts. If they fade into the deep timber with the boy, I'll never see him again."

"I need to have a good horse. I'll go in the morning at first light, Miss Gordon."

CHAPTER 6

His nose tingled from the smell of fresh-baked bread even before he saw the outline of the woman standing in the barn doorway holding a saddled horse.

"I hope this mare will do, Mr. Paintier. I've been keeping her hidden from the raiders," she said.

"Looks like a fine bay to me."

"There's a loaf of bread in the saddlebags and some fried-up bacon wrapped up with it for when you get hungry."

"Thank you, ma'am,"

"Can you find him, Mr. Paintier?"

"I don't know, Miss Gordon."

Nelson grabbed the carbine from the corner of the barn, opened the breach, and chambered a cartridge. He pointed it out the barn door, aiming across the iron sights, and then lowered the hammer before dropping the loaded weapon into the scabbard. He drew the .44, spun the cylinder, checked for loads, and then slipped it back into his hip holster.

Nelson tugged the saddle horn, and easily slipped his fingers under the girth. The bay had sucked in a big breath when it had been saddled, so Nelson walked the horse outside and pulled the slack out of the girth. He dropped the stirrups two holes lower to match his six-foot, three-inch frame, slipped his left foot in the stirrup and mounted the horse.

It took only a glance at the path outside the barn for Nelson to tell the direction the boy and mule were headed.

"I see where he went. It looks like back toward the ironworks. Any idea where he might go from there?"

"Mr. Paintier, Joshua's dad has come back only a few times since he had troubles with my sister," she said.

"Has his dad talked any, I mean about quitting the bushwhackers and coming back to Steelville?" Nelson asked.

"I think he would fancy having a wife and family. Union troops have been close to catching his bunch more than one time. He said last time he was here several of the men riding with him wanted to quit and come home."

"I'll be checking the ironworks first, but doubt if Joshua knows where to go from there. I think the best cover for a bushwhacker would be deep in the Huzzah cave areas."

"Bring him home, Mr. Paintier."

"Nelson, just Nelson."

"May God guide you and bring you both back safely, Nelson," Ruth Anne said.

As he crossed the flat leading into the ironworks, he saw his mule tied in front of the blacksmith's shop. The smithy looked up, holding a steel rod with a bright orange tip in the air; it had just come out of his charcoal fired forge.

"Boy said you would be coming for the mule. He tied it to the post when he couldn't get it to leave here, and took off walking west along the Stringtown Road. Been gone about four hours now," the blacksmith said. "Where's he headed?"

"Looking for something he's lost," Nelson replied. "You can have the mule to keep. I'll get the saddle on the way back."

"Best you keep the carbine in your lap while traveling toward Rolla. Bushwhackers keep outriders posted along the trace in that direction."

"Thanks. If the boy shows up back here, see if you can keep him around until I get back," Nelson said.

Nelson turned the bay and spurred it into a lope up the narrow wagon path they called the Stringtown Road. The rocky ridgeback trail showed no signs of footprints; he could only hope to spot the boy ahead.

Nelson drew the winded bay to a walk, to cool the mare out, after an hours ride. Sure the boy hadn't gotten that far, Nelson turned back.

Slowed to a walk, he saw a broken branch at rider level. Someone had ridden off the trace and into the woods. He slipped his foot out of the stirrup and slid to the ground to check a well-worn deer trail that led south. He ran his fingers over the many scratches he saw on the rocks. Horseshoes. Riders had turned off the trace and headed southeast toward the Huzzah River basin.

The isolated trail and the cover it provided convinced him the riders had been guerrilla raiders. Nelson put his foot in the stirrup and eased back into the saddle.

He lightly touched the bay's side with his heels and turned past the broken twig down the deer trail going south. It would be dark in a couple of hours. The thought of being on the guerrilla's trail in the darkness made his spine tingle his arm twitch, He was reminded of Rebel sharpshooters who'd wait for his kind of fool during the war.

Boulders the size of log cabins lined the edges of the trail as it wound toward the Huzzah basin. A thick forest covered the trail, keeping out the little light that still remained of the day. Nelson knew the horse would follow the narrow trail on its own when full darkness came.

A slight breeze from the west crossed his path as darkness fell. Twice within the last few minutes he stopped the bay to listen for sounds that were masked by the squeaks of his saddle, and the short sniffing breaths of the horse. The third time, he pulled up suddenly, but still he couldn't pinpoint any pursuer. He turned off the trail to his right and stopped the bay. Rubbing the horse's neck didn't help to quiet the nervous animal.

He took one foot from the stirrup and stood to swing his leg to dismount. At that moment, the panther attacked. Claws raked across the horse's rump as the predator crashed against Nelson's back, knocking him out of the saddle and flat on the ground. Nelson sprang to his knees and reached to draw his .44. The holster hung empty at his side. He heard tree branches snap as the stampeding horse bucked to throw off the demon on its back and then the sound of the horse running hard back up the trail toward the trace. The crunch of dry leaves directly in front of him sent tremors through his gut. The panther's guttural snarl came from close to his left, it was moving slowly around him. He knew the attack would come when the cat grew tired of tormenting its trapped quarry. Nelson turned to follow the sounds and face the coming attack. He swept his hand out over the ground in front, feeling for the big Griswold .44. He froze when a wet blast of spittle, from the cat, peppered his hand and arm. The animal's hesitation to attack convinced Nelson he might have a chance to avoid being eaten alive.

He picked up two rocks, he had tripped over, and tried to guess how far away the snarling panther was poised. *Oh, the hell with it!* He crashed the rocks together, stomped his feet, and ran at the panther with the blood curdling yell the Rebs had used to scare the hell out of him. He heard the thrashing of the big cat's paws as it recoiled at the sudden attack from the strange prey. He threw both rocks at the cat's sounds, heard them thump flesh, and then backed off from his feigned attack to wait. He heard only the wind; the panther had pulled back.

It took Nelson only a few seconds of sweeping his foot over the ground to find his pistol. Holding the .44 pointed toward the last place he had heard the panther; he backed off the trail and against a boulder. The security of the cocked pistol in his hand helped to cut down the churning in his empty stomach.

His worry about the lost pardons and finding Joshua had taken first priority over eating the fresh-baked bread stored in the saddlebags of a horse that must still be running, headed toward the safety of its barn. Thinking of greener pastures, the beautiful woman back in Steelville didn't help his hurting back. Being pressed up against some cold rock in guerrilla territory waiting for an enemy blacker than night, wanting nothing more than to eat him, was hardly encouraging. Things were happening too fast, he'd wanted to spend a few weeks in his hometown talking to the old timers and then try to arrange a meeting with some of the guerrilla leaders for a sit-down.

His worry increased when he heard the clatter of two horses coming up the rocky trail from the south. He heard the heavy breathing of the two horses as the riders went by and stopped a short distance up the trail. Nelson heard them talking but couldn't make out what they were saying. He heard the horses coming back toward him at a slow walk.

"Hey, Johnny Reb. We heard you yelping up here."

"Whats you hollering like that fer? Come on out; we's your friends."

Nelson realized if he didn't come out the two men would have their whole band out beating the brush for him in the morning.

"I'm here. Panther jumped me. I think I scared his black hide off with that yell."

The two men dismounted and stood behind their horses, looking in the direction of Nelson's voice.

"We can't see much of you, mister. If you be packin' best give it to Charley here."

"Can't see you neither. Reckon I won't be giving up this .44 to somebody could be a Yankee."

"Hell, man. Me and Charley be about as far from a Yankee as we can get. Come on out, and we'll take you to meet the rest of our boys."

" 'Spect you ain't Yankees. Lost my horse, so I need to double up."

"You can ride behind Charley, he's the little one. For me, mister, gonna' need that .44. Boys will skin me alive if I bring a stranger in camp carrying a pistol."

Nelson reluctantly gave up his pistol to the guerrilla and mounted up behind Charley. They turned down the trail toward the south.

"Ain't far, mister. Couple of our boys was sitting on the cliff over the cave when they heard you yell."

Nelson hadn't planned to be thrown in with the guerrillas this quickly. He knew it would take some leg flipping, jig dancing to get out of this hornet's nest alive.

The ride down to the river took only a few minutes. They turned west along the bank of the Meramec and then up a steep hill to dismount at the mouth of a cave. It didn't surprise Nelson, no cooking fires were burning; they were hunted men hiding from the federal troops. Charley led Nelson to the back wall and a flat spot with an empty blanket.

"Place for tonight. Morning we going to get a better look at you. Figure out what the hell you want, coming down that trail in the dark."

Nelson couldn't argue with a cave full of bushwhackers. He had tried to get an exact count of how many men were bunked in the cave but it was too dark, so he stretched out on the hard cave floor to catch his breath and rest. He could just make out the two men on the way toward him.

"Stand up, mister."

The two men grabbed Nelson's coat and yanked him to his feet, pulling his arms behind him, to tie them.

"Charley thought it would be fine, just leaving you sitting here. We don't think so. Want to know who you are and why you followed this trail."

"Name's Nelson Paintier. Started this morning from Steelville looking for a boy. He ran off last night. I had found him the first time in the middle of the river on top of his house with his mother. I was lucky to save the boy. Took him home to Steelville."

"Was it your boy?"

"Nope. Boy's name is Joshua Spencer."

"Gonna tie you right out front to that oak tree, so you get a good look at that river, in the morning. Same river we goin' t' drown your lying ass in, 'fore noon."

The two men yanked Nelson off his feet and dragged him across the cave to the big oak tree in front.

"We don't take to no strangers coming down that trail."

"Told you, looking for the boy. That's all. Panther ran off my horse, or I'd be gone."

"Don't do no good making up shit stories. Gonna kill you anyway."

CHAPTER 7

Nelson didn't like his second time of spending the night against a tree any more than the first. Dawn showed the Meramec River running clear as glass.

He watched a beaver's wake as it carried a large willow branch toward a deep cut in the bank. He'd never gotten over the way he killed the first beaver he trapped in the Meramec when he was a boy. The drowning stake for his beaver set hadn't worked. The big beaver circled the tie staking, dragging the double jaw trap on its hind foot. Nelson tried to push it to the bottom and drown it. Up the beaver would come, and he would have to try again. He wanted to kill it fast so it wouldn't suffer. He could think of no way to get the trap off the animal in the water. Finally, when the beaver's head came up for air, Nelson hit toward it with a stout club. The beaver dove again. The next time it came up, Nelson struck hard. The beaver's nose shattered and it swam in a darkening circle of blood. Two more times he struck at the shattered nose and head. Finally the beaver rolled over and floated to the top of the water. Nelson removed the beaver from the trap and carried him to the bank. Nelson waded back to the water-set and removed the stake and trap for good. When he looked back, the shattered beaver had crawled to the edge of the river, trying to reach the safety of the water. This time Nelson's blow killed the animal. He felt sick.

The thought crossed his mind more than once during the night that he could be down there under the water fighting for his breath before the day ended. He had enough looking at rivers to last a good long time, and the thought of going back in the Meramec, this time head down, gave him a head ache.

Just before dawn Nelson saw a rider leave, cross the river, and head south. The rest of the men were stirring in the cave. They still had built no cook fires. Nelson tried to twist around the tree to watch the bushwhackers behind him.

"Next time I see that head come around the tree, I'm going to shoot it off."

Three of the men were headed toward the oak. One with a carbuncled face stood with his nose pressing tight to the side of Nelson's face.

"Want to tell us again, 'bout what you're doing on this here trail?"

"Told you, looking for a boy," Nelson said.

"Untie him. Gonna take him for his last swim."

Nelson knew too well the ruthlessness of the guerrillas holding out in the southern Missouri hills. He knew they wouldn't need a reason to kill him. The men dragged him down the steep slope toward the cold Meramec waters.

"Tie that rope 'round his feet. Throw it over the limb hanging out over the water. Gonna sink that lying head deep."

The men pulled the rope tight and lifted Nelson across the top of the water into a head-down position.

"Sink him; sink his sorry ass," the bushwhacker said.

Nelson sucked in the deepest breath his lungs would hold before his head went under. He needed it all before they lifted him back out again.

"Gonna give you a last chance, here, mister. You been spying on us, haven't you?"

"Told you, look-"

Nelson took a mouth full of water on the last word. He held back the impulse to choke until his lungs emptied. The cough that followed filled his throat and windpipe with water. Still they didn't lift him. *Nelson saw the beaver with the crushed nose swimming in a bloody circle before he passed out.*

"Shit! I think we killed the bastard."

Nelson felt the slaps and heard the voices trying to bring him back to consciousness.

"What boy? What boy were you looking for?"

"Steelville boy."

"Tell him what boy. His name?"

"Joshua . . . Joshua . . . Spencer," Nelson said.

Nelson sat up back on the riverbank with several of the raiders kneeling around him.

"Somebody just got here wants to know why you were looking for Joshua."

"He ran off. Looking for his dad."

One of the men pushed to Nelson's side, "They told me you saved my boy from the flood. Ain't no loss if that whore wife of mine is drowned, but the boy, he was okay?" Dyer Spencer asked.

"He was yesterday morning. Lost his track after the ironworks; I'm sure he was coming looking for his pa," Nelson said getting to his feet.

"He may still be up on the trace. Saddle up. We're going to tie you back up so you'll be handy to drown if we don't find my boy," Dyer said.

The sun had dropped behind the river bluff when the riders returned. Nelson didn't see Joshua until he slid off the back of his dad's horse. Dyer cut Nelson's ropes and took him to the front of the cave to join the boy. Joshua smiled when he saw Nelson walking toward him.

"You know we kill strangers in these here parts. They don't have half the chance of a fat boar pig at a hog roast," Dyer said.

"Is that what happened to a certain Union officer and his escort troops a while back?" Nelson asked.

"Is that what folk are saying about me and the boys?"

"Don't matter to me what you've done, Spencer. God damn war is nearly over now."

"Ain't over for us till we say so, mister. Some of the boys caught those Yankee troops right after they hanged Ralph Biggs. Troops had pulled him out of his house and strung him up in the yard right in front of his wife and kids. Bastards looking to loot his place," Dyer said.

"Should have turned them in to the troop headquarters at Rolla."

"They'd a shot us before we got to the fort gate. Nobody can do no wrong down here, but us Rebs."

"Don't think about coming home? Being a father to the boy?" Nelson asked.

"Thought about it some. Don't do no good thinking about something that ain't gonna happen," Spencer said.

"Nobody at the ironworks talked about any money being offered on your head, Spencer. The money is all being offered on Anderson and his bunch."

Nelson had given Dyer Spencer something to think about. Dyer and the boy left and walked to the front of the cave and sat talking. Soon Nelson saw Dyer give his son a hug and then head back.

"The boy can't stay. It's not safe for him to be with us. There are still some troops from out of Rolla looking for us. Take the boy back to Miss Gordon. Ask her to look after his schooling and give him a place to live. You can head out in the morning."

"You fellows didn't happen to find my bay horse up on the trace, did you?" asked Nelson.

"Joshua had it. He caught the mare coming down the trace right after dark. Some of the boys got her, rubbing some hog grease on the cuts on its flank. Lucky that big cat didn't have you for his supper," Dyer said.

"Scared me so bad I didn't want any supper."

"Nelson, thanks for saving my boy. He told me how you rode into the river and lost your horse and all. Be proud to have you come back and join up with us. Talk is we might head down into Arkansas."

"I'll take him back, Dyer. Won't be joining you now, though. Got some things to settle yet in Steelville," Nelson said.

"They brought your saddle and an extra blanket by the back wall there. Curl up till morning. I'll have Joshua bring you the .44 in the morning, that way my boys won't be nervous about you having it while they sleep," Dyer said.

The dirt floor of the cave would feel like a feather bed after the previous couple of days. With the saddle as his pillow, he knew rest would finally come. He heard a rider coming up the trail from the river going hard. It didn't matter.

"Wake up, Nelson. Damn it to hell, Nelson. Wake up," Dyer kicked his saddle.

"They got Union Troops sitting all along the river with their rifles pointing up here just waiting for morning. Must have followed us when we were looking for the boy," Dyer said.

Nelson shook off the deep sleep.

"Get the bay saddled," Dyer said.

Nelson knew it wouldn't matter who he had helped win the war. To the rifles waiting out front he would be just another bushwhacker. Shooting their way out while riding breakneck down a steep hill would cost more than half of Dyer's men.

"Keep Joshua with you, Nelson. We got to hope those Yankees don't know about the back entrance to this cave and how we are going to ride out of it, a long way back up the ridge at daybreak," Dyer said. "When we get out we're going to lead them away from you and the boy. Take 'em out five or six mile, and turn on them when the land is good for a fight."

Single file the men and horses led the way through the cave passages. Three of the men carried oil-soaked torches that came into view when the passage straightened out. Each man held the tail of the horse in front of him, to lead the way through the blackness.

He heard the splashing of water and felt the cold as their path took them through a shallow underground river. Out of the water, the air got colder, moving around them and coming from somewhere up ahead. The line stopped, and the torches were put out. No one spoke; not a horse whinnied, a well-trained army of men and animals. Nelson guessed that pickets were being sent forward out of the cave checking for Union soldiers. The line moved again, up a steep, narrow passage that broke out of the cave on the high ridge behind it. The line of men and horses walked on for more than a hundred yards and then stopped to mount. Nelson saw Dyer headed for him and the boy.

"When you hit the trace up ahead, turn right and ride like hell. We're going to circle back and give those troopers some hell, draw them off west behind us. Take good care of my son, Nelson. I won't forget you saving him from the flood," Dyer said. "So long, son."

Only the soft squeaks of worn saddles and the brushing sound of the horse's tails whisking across their rumps gave away their leaving the cave on the ride north, up the trail, past the boulder where the panther had attacked. The lead riders broke out on to the Rolla trace when the shooting started, an ambush the bushwhackers didn't expect. The guerilla riders circled back and then spread to the right and left of the deer trail in a skirmish line. They advanced at a gallop on the ambushers waiting on the road. A blood-curdling Rebel yell broke out to Nelson's right and spread across the line of bushwhackers. Nelson rode at the back of the advancing line and heard the shots first from the Union riders who came up behind them from the river.

He yelled to warn Spencer and turned to see two in the lead charging headlong toward him, firing as they came. He slapped Joshua's horse on the rump and drew his .44. Dyer shot first and one rider went down. The second trooper fell from a .44 lead bullet through his chest. Nelson watched the blue uniformed trooper tumble from his horse and looked in disbelief at the smoking .44 in his right hand.

"I'm hit, Nelson," yelled Dyer.

Nelson spurred his horse to Dyer's side. Joshua followed close behind.

"Took one in the shoulder," Dyer slumped in his saddle.

"Let me help my dad," Joshua said.

"Stay mounted, son. Follow up quick," Nelson said, headed east into the heavy brush.

"I'll try to stay with you," shouted Dyer.

Nelson reined the horse off the traveled trail and into the timber. He tried to pick a path around the fallen limbs and rotten logs so the wounded Dyer could follow without falling off his horse. When his horse jumped a dead tree, Nelson looked back to see if Dyer made it across. The wounded man leaned forward over the saddle horn, holding on with his good arm and following close behind.

"Keep going. Go harder, Nelson," yelled Dyer. "They'll have scouts looking for us when the shooting stops."

Nelson quickened the pace and pushed aside the low limbs that grabbed and scratched at his head and arms.

They were traveling on the side of a razorback ridge with narrow breaks that dropped so steeply the horses kept sliding down the side. The struggle to climb back out slowed the pace. As the ridge got steeper Nelson had to lean forward over the horse's neck to keep it from going over backward.

"I don't see him, Nelson," Joshua said. "He was right behind us."

"There's a stand of cedars ahead. We can wait, let him catch up there," Nelson said.

"There he comes," Joshua said.

Dyer's riderless horse struggled up the steep bank behind them and trotted to the side of the other two horses before stopping. The saddle and the side of the horse were covered with mud and dirt. Nelson guessed the horse had fallen climbing out of the gullies they'd crossed.

"Slide down and grab the horse, Joshua. I'll go back for him," Nelson said.

Nelson found Dyer slowly climbing up the edge of the last steep ridge break.

"Take Joshua and get out of here, Paintier," Dyer said.

"He's waiting up ahead. He caught your horse. He won't leave without you. Come on."

He cleared a stirrup for Dyer's foot and lifted him by his good arm to the back of his saddle. Back at the cedars Joshua pushed his dad's horse over next to a log, so his dad could climb back into his own saddle.

"Get me to Stringtown, Paintier. I've got friends there," Dyer said.

Nelson took the reins to lead Dyer's horse, then headed along the ridge again toward the ironworks and Stringtown. Dyer told him the troops wouldn't be following on the steep and dangerous ridge path.

They approached Stringtown from the valley side of the open pit iron mine at the crest of Stringtown Road. Nelson stopped the horses out of sight of the mine and dismounted.

"Joshua, ride your horse past the iron mine down the Stringtown Road. Don't stop at the cabin your pa told us about. Ride on past to the bottom of the hill. Circle back from there. We'll wait here for you," Nelson said. "See if there are any Union troops along the Stringtown Road."

"What if they are there?" Joshua asked.

"Ride by them and head straight for your aunt's," Nelson said. "I'll take care of getting your dad someplace safe."

More than two hours passed, and Joshua hadn't returned. The troops had to be searching the Stringtown cabins for the guerrillas. Nelson bandaged Dyer's wound, and the bleeding slowed from the pressure he kept on it. They sat hidden in the thick brush until darkness came.

"Let's get you up on this horse, Dyer. We're going to head around the ironworks. I know a place not far from here where you can hide till that wound stops bleeding and I can get some water and grub for you," Nelson said, helping Dyer get on his horse.

In less than an hour they reached the empty dogtrot cabin Nelson's father had built. Nelson took Dyer around the cabin to a shed built on a rock wall foundation. Inside he motioned for Dyer to stand back. Using his buck knife Nelson pried away the loose boards in the floor to reveal a large iron gate cover. He struggled to lift the hinged cover nearly frozen in place with rust, and motioned for Dyer.

"There are steps going down, and ledges on each side where the slaves slept. Owner locked them down here for the night. No one will find you here," Nelson said.

He went down the steps with Dyer's arm over his shoulder and lowered him to one of the rock ledges.

"It's too dark to see much, does feel like your shoulder has stopped bleeding."

"Think the shot went clean through," Dyer said.

"Going to leave you some hardtack. I'll come back tomorrow to take care of your wound."

Nelson remembered the bacon and bread in the saddlebags and went to fetch it and water the horses. He took the horses down the hill to the spring pool and stood watching them drink.

The memory of the day he caused the baby to drown in the spring pool would never stop haunting him. Mary had been a good nurse to the baby, always watching it, keeping it away from the spring. A young boy teasing the fourteen-year-old girl had distracted her for just those few minutes. After her trial, he had tried to tell them, she didn't drown the baby. His pleading for her came too late.

He tied the horses in the woods and went back to the slave-pit hiding place. He gave Dyer the food and a canteen of water. At the top of pit, he closed the grate and covered the pit with loose boards.

"Damn, Nelson! You come back. Don't you leave me in this shit hole place."

"I'll be back tomorrow, right now have to go and get some bandages for you."

He hadn't told Dyer about the lost saddlebags he needed to find. Nelson flexed the horse around the thick brush and trees that lined the south banks of the Meramec River. The search for his old horse, Blue, and the saddlebags took him through the mud and around the trash left by the flood. He rode past a group of townspeople probing and stooping to search the piles of brush left by the high water. They told him the count of missing and dead had climbed to more than twenty. He didn't ask if they had found the mare.

When he rode past another brush pile, he found his warhorse. The mare lay half covered in the mud. When he tried to get closer, the bay shied at the dead horse. Nelson forced his horse to circle the dead mare.

Nelson sucked a deep chest-raiser breath. "Oh, shit!"

The saddlebags were gone and a lone set of footprints led off toward the ironworks. Following the tracks in the muddy river bottom would be easy.

Nelson swept his hat across his chest in a last salute to his dead warhorse. "Sorry, Blue. There are still battles I have to fight."

He turned the horse slowly and then kicked into a fast walk to follow the tracks. The tracks circled several large heaps of trash and brush before continuing in the direction of the ironworks and Stringtown. When the tracks left the muddy river bottom and joined a wagon road, Nelson lost the trail. He circled back a ways to get a closer look at the unevenness in the two footprints and then turned toward the dogtrot cabin to pick up Dyer's horse. Who ever found the saddlebags walked with a bad limp.

CHAPTER 8

When Nelson rode into the barnyard at daylight, leading Dyer's horse, Joshua stuck his straw covered head out of the haymow door. "The troops were searching the cabins in Stringtown. I couldn't get back. Is my dad safe?"

"He's safe for now," Nelson replied.

"He got shot. Is he going to be okay?"

"I'm going back, take some clean bandages and food for him," climbing down from his saddle.

"Can I go?" Joshua asked.

"I'm going alone this time. In a couple of days when he's better, you can go see him."

Nelson slipped the saddles off the horses and led them to the rear stall in the barn. He ran his hand over the deep scratches the panther had ripped in the bay's haunches. He would darn sure put a quick release tie on his holster before he went on another night ride in Ozark panther country. He had felt naked searching for the .44 in the darkness.

"Joshua, could you slide some hay down? Feed the horses for me."

"Sure. Oh, my aunt said two men were here yesterday. She said they were nosing around asking questions about the stranger."

"Thanks, Joshua."

"She wanted you to come to the house when you got back."

"Is she up yet?" Nelson asked.

"I saw her feeding the chickens, a while ago."

Nelson needed rest, but worried about the men asking questions. Could they have found his saddlebags and the pardons? He climbed the two steps, crossed Ruth Anne's porch and knocked. He turned at the clanging of a can at the back of the house, and looked over the edge of the porch railing.

"Mr. Paintier," Ruth Anne said. She closed the gate to the chicken coop, set the feed bucket on the ground and joined Nelson at the front of the house.

"Miss Gordon, I rode in a few minutes ago and wanted to tell you about the boy's dad."

"Joshua told me his dad was injured. I was sorry we had to bury his mother before he got back. I told him we just couldn't wait for him."

"I'm sorry I couldn't get him back in time."

"I think he understood, Mr. Paintier, it helped that he got to see his father," Ruth Anne said.

"Dyer got it in the shoulder. I found a place for him to hide at the cabin my father and I built."

"Joshua told me his dad got shot in the ambush. Is he going to be okay?"

"He needs to see a doctor, but he won't let me see to getting one for him. I'll just have to do my best to treat the wound." Nelson asked if she would get together some bandages later that day for him to take to Dyer when it got dark. He didn't want to alarm her about the men asking questions so he didn't ask about them right then. He needed to find a place to stay, away from her house and school so she would be safe.

"I'm going to walk through town this morning. See what's left down there," Nelson said.

"I'll have the bandages ready for you this afternoon," Ruth Anne said.

"If the boy could scrape off some red-oak bark we can mix it with water for a disinfectant. It'll help to hurry up healing Dyer's wound."

"I'm sure he would love to help his father," she said.

Nelson walked down the hill past the school house to the valley floor. Down along the creek he passed the rocks that had supported the general store and remembered the winter nights when the old timers sat with their feet against the pot-bellied stove and telling wild tales about when they were boys. He avoided the courthouse and waded across Yadkin Creek. He walked toward a man and woman prying boards off their wrecked home; it had been pushed from its foundation by the water.

"Expect I could give you folks a hand. If you'd let me?" Nelson said.

"Ain't no hurry getting it done. Least ways not till winter gets here," the man rested the head of his axe on a log.

The woman clamped both her hands to her hips, "Might not be so in a man's eye. We can't sleep in this wreck of a house waiting for another flood to come; wash us clean away."

"I can give you a hand with that board, ma'am." Nelson pulled the broken board from the house framing.

The woman said, "We went to bury Mrs. Spencer yesterday. Ruth Anne said your father was Levi Lane Paintier. Both of us knew you and your dad."

"I thought I remembered you. Would it be, let's see, Ellis and May Oliver?"

"You do remember," May Oliver said.

"I do ma'am. My dad always said you were probably kin folks."

"We always wondered what happened to you, Nelson. Thought you might have been killed the same night as your dad," Ellis said.

"The riders that burned our house tried to kill me. I hid and headed out of here the day after they hanged the slave girl," Nelson said.

"You know it seemed peculiar. The fire that killed your dad, night before they hung that terrible girl," Ellis said.

"It was more than peculiar, Ellis," Nelson said.

"Where you been all this time, Nelson?" May asked.

Nelson took a deep breath before answering quietly, "Traveling a bit, fighting a war, May."

Ellis replied first, "You don't have to say that in a whisper, Nelson. May and me, we wanted to leave things as they were before the war. A lot of the folks here feel the same way."

May stood with her hands on her hips again looking at Nelson. "We've been beat on by both sides. Yankees stomp in here and burn folks out if they think they have been helping the rebels. The damn rebels come at us out of the woods, more bushwhackers than soldiers, I'd say. Kill and loot folks for no reason at all. So it don't matter which side you fought on, both just as bad as the other. Lots of folks here hate the bushwhackers more than they do the Yankees."

"I understand what you are saying, Mrs. Oliver. We can all pray that the madness ends soon. By the way, you didn't happen to see a couple fellows riding through here asking questions about me, did you?" Nelson asked.

"Them fellows stopped up at the teacher's house and then rode off. We didn't see them up close," Ellis said.

"You might ask Ned Gunther, he was up on the ridge when they went by. They stopped to talk to him for a couple minutes," May said. "He lives in the last house, before heading on the trace to the ironworks."

"I think I'll head up there. Would like to know who's asking about me," Nelson said.

"We're glad to see you back, Nelson," May said. She waved goodbye to him.

Nelson climbed the hill, and turned around near the top to study the washed-out valley and what remained of the courthouse and the sheriff's office below. He hated the sheriff for beating the confession out of the slave girl. He hated his dad for the beating he got for wanting to tell what happened. Most of all Nelson hated himself for not saving the girl.

He guessed the man working in the garden alongside the trace would be Gunther.

"Howdy. Would you happen to be Ned Gunther?" Nelson asked.

"Aye, and would you be the Paintier boy those fellows were asking about?"

"I'm afraid I would be. Did you know those fellows, Mr. Gunther?"

"One of them was an older fellow I remembered seeing in town," Gunther said.

"They didn't say their name?" asked Nelson.

"The younger fellow called the older man Jasper."

"It looks like the rain washed away your plantings."

"I have to keep working, trying to plant a garden in this here darn clay. Nothing wants to grow like in the old country. Best growing is down in the valley if there's any good dirt left."

Nelson thanked Gunther and started the walk back along the ridge to the barn. He still was thinking about the name Jasper, when he heard the running horses behind him. When the horses slid to a stop, Nelson turned to face the riders.

"Come back, have you, Paintier," said the man to Nelson's right.

"Came back to stay," Nelson said, resting his hand on his pistol.

"Spaid said he don't want you here, waking up sleeping black bears," the man said. "Might get a schoolteacher killed."

"Why don't you start the killing with me, you son-of-a-bitch," Nelson said.

Both of the riders reached for their pistols at the same time. Nelson's first shot got the man on the right in the shoulder before his pistol could be aimed. His second shot hit the other man's pistol; it went flying out of his shattered hand before he could fire.

"Hold those horses still, damn you. Tell Spaid he's a dead man, and Nelson Paintier said so. Now, get the hell out of here. I'll kill you both if you ever come back."

CHAPTER 9

Ruth Anne stood in the school yard holding a slate tablet when Nelson came down the hill after the shots were fired.

"Let's go inside, Ruth Anne," said Nelson. They walked to the front of the one room schoolhouse and sat on the edge of the raised platform in front of the blackboard.

"Mr. Paintier, you need to tell me what's going on. Those riders, up on the ridge? Did you kill that man?"

"No, but I shot both of them up some, before they could kill me. They were sent by the man that killed my dad, the night before they hung the slave girl."

"What's the slave girl got to do with you?" standing and going to her desk to lay the tablet on top.

"I knew the slave girl, Ruth Anne. It was as much my fault as hers that the Mockbee baby drowned," Nelson said, going to the side of Ruth Anne's desk to face her.

"I went to Sheriff Spaid and told him I was there when the baby drowned. Told him it was my fault. He laughed at me, and called me a nigger lover. Said for me to go home before someone hung me instead of the girl."

"But, Nelson the slave girl confessed to killing the baby. The town celebrated the day they hung her every year, before the war came."

"I was hiding in the woods when the men came for her. They took her in back of the cabin, tied her to a tree and beat her till she had to confess."

"Why didn't you tell them what happened?" Ruth Anne asked.

"I've tried for years to find excuses for not saving her. None have helped me forget. I went to my dad and told him what had happened. When he found out I had been playing with a slave girl at the spring pool he beat me. I was afraid of him."

"You went to the sheriff? Why didn't you speak up at the trial for her?"

"It wasn't a trial. It was a lynching from the first word said."

"Is this why you came back here?" Ruth Anne asked. "You must still feel guilty for her hanging."

"I've felt guilty for her getting hanged ever since the day I left. In my mind I've watched Sheriff Spaid drag her up the steps of the gallows over and over again. I've watched her eyes race across the hate filled faces staring up at her, before they pulled the cover over her head. She had been looking, trying to find my face in the crowd. I may have been the only friend she had ever known."

Ruth Anne came around the desk, closer to Nelson. She rested her hand on his shoulder.

"It's not your fault, Nelson. With things like they were then. She was black, a slave. That was enough for any jury to hang her. It's still that way, Nelson. It's still that way."

"I guess what happened to a slave girl was a lot of the reason I fought for the North, Ruth Anne. I'm sorry I didn't tell you sooner."

"I guessed it the first day I met you, Nelson."

"I came back to tell her story. The people here need to know what happened. I started writing it during the war and it's nearly finished. I left most of the manuscript in safe hands in Saint Louis. It's the story of the ironworks, the slaves who worked there, and the days a white boy and black girl spent playing by the spring pool on the hillside by the dogtrot cabin my father and I built."

"Nelson, when people learn you fought for the North they will probably want to hang you too."

"I'll have to go down fighting. I intend to stay. It's not those people I'm worried about. It's the men that threw flaming bottles on our roof and through our windows. The man that killed my dad, he's still here. That's why the riders came to kill me. He knows I'll be looking for him."

"I think you should be very careful what you do here, Nelson. Some people hate the Union soldiers even more than they hate the colored folks."

"Ruth Anne, the family in Saint Louis who took me in as their son owned a newspaper. They taught me the business. With the money they left me when they died, I plan to start the first Crawford County newspaper."

"You're serious?"

"I am. I've several things to finish up before it gets started."

"This town is going to need all the help it can get to rebuild the businesses that were lost," Ruth Anne said. "A newspaper would be a great help to bring new people into the county and the Meramec Valley."

"I hope you're right. I'd better be heading back to where Dyer is holed up. If you have the things ready I'd like to get started, Ruth Anne."

"They're ready. Would you like to just call me Anne?"

"I would . . . Anne."

"Stay safe, Nelson. We need the likes of you in our county."

"There is another reason why I came back, Anne." Nelson explained the orders his Saint Louis commander had asked him to carry out, and told her how the pardons had been lost in the flood. Anne seemed relieved a pardon would allow Dyer to someday feel safe to come back and be a father to Joshua.

Nelson saddled the horse and hung the sack with the food and bandages across the saddle horn. He had several stops to make along the trace before darkness came. He wanted to know where to find the ex-sheriff John Spaid. He had hoped someone had shot the sonofabitch to save him the trouble of doing it. Nelson made his first stop at the side of the gardener's house.

Gunther stood in the front yard of his house. "Saw those riders come back. It was bad luck for them, picking a gun fight with you."

"Guess I came out the winner from that fight."

"I remember where I saw the one called Jasper."

"Where was that, Mr. Gunther?"

"It was at the capital, Jefferson City. I came on a ferryboat from Saint Louis with my cousin. He just arrived from Germany. The man saw his suitcase and started yelling at him about being a dirty German. That's where I saw him, hanging around the state capitol building."

"Thanks, Gunther. Do you have any idea what he was doing up there at the capitol?"

"I don't know, mister. He did have some kind of a badge on. That's the only reason my cousin didn't knock his block off."

"One more question, Mr. Gunther. Do you know what might have happened to John Spaid?"

"Don't know about that, but there is an old lady lives up the South Creek branch, about four miles back in there, is where she lives. Her name is Spaid, I go back to see her now and then."

After thanking Gunther again, Nelson headed over the ridge to the South Creek trail. Spaid's connection with the state capitol bothered him. Why would the men come from there to kill him?

The trail sat tucked between a bluff and the small stream someone had named South Creek. It had been a roaring river a few days before. The trail was shaded by pin oak trees, Nelson knew the hundred-year-old trees were there when he first came to Crawford County. He guided the bay around the many broken pin oak limbs lying across the narrow trail. In the patches of sunlight Nelson saw snakes coil when he approached, their bronze coats warned him to stay clear of the poisonous copperheads.

A loud squeal from the brush alongside the trail surprised him, his horse shied and spun away from the sound. He lost the right stirrup and sat crooked in the saddle until he pulled the horse's head hard in the direction of the spin, to stop it from running away.

Still squealing, a frightened old sow with two of her litter dangling from her teats ran up the hill toward an old vine-covered cabin. Eight babies followed, they tripped and rolled over each other all the way to the house.

"Last person scared my sow I took a shot at him and blowed half the leaves off that dogwood you sitting by. Any reason I shouldn't do the same for you, mister?"

The woman who stood by the cabin held about the oldest blunderbuss shotgun Nelson had ever seen. The pair of men's pants she had on looked big enough for at least two of her, a strand of cotton rope tied at her side held them up. Her gray hair hung straight on each side of the slender face. Nelson thought, yes, she belonged with a vine covered cabin.

"Mrs. Spaid?" Nelson asked, still trying to get straight in the saddle.

"Least you know my name. Reckon you're not out here to rob an old woman."

"Reckon not ma'am."

"Ride on up here. Speak what's on your mind, and don't call me Spaid, my name is Jenny. Just Jenny."

"I'm from these parts, Jenny. Been gone since before the war," Nelson got off his horse.

"You ain't one of them Yankees are you mister? Be a shame to have to shoot a man that's as good lookin' as you."

Nelson chuckled and didn't answer her question. He let it pass.

"Spent all the war living up here along this creek. Didn't know what was going on, except when I had to go to town for salt and foodstuff. Raised most of what I eat right here."

"Back about fifteen years ago I knew John Spaid, is he your husband?"

"Asking about the high and mighty Sheriff John Spaid, are you! No, he weren't no husband of mine. At one time 'fore he got to be sheriff, he was my brother."

Nelson wasn't sure how to ask the next question. He guessed the old lady would answer it without being asked anyway.

"Mister, if you're looking for him so you can shoot him, tell him Jenny Spaid told you where to find him. Last I heard he was living in the hills south of Jeff."

"You have a lot of hate for someone that's your kin," Nelson said.

"I suppose you can say I do. He killed the only man I ever really loved, just cause he didn't like him. Said if I ever told anybody about things he done, his boys would be sent out here and kill me too. So I ain't never told, just wrote myself notes about all he did. It'll be a cold spring 'fore he ever finds them. Kill the bastard and come back, I'll tell you all he's done. Make the hair stand up all along your neck."

"If I find him, I'll tell him you send your best wishes."

"Best wishes that he's dead, good lookin'," she chuckled.

CHAPTER 10

Nelson left Jenny sitting in a willow limb chair beside her cabin. He liked the old woman and knew how much fun it would be to tell her he had shot Sheriff John Spaid. He was sure she had a jug of moonshine saved for just that occasion. Nelson knew anyone else with that much dirt on Sheriff Spaid would already be dead.

He looked forward to a faceoff with Spaid, but his orders came first. Nelson backtracked down the creek past the copperheads and headed down the trace toward the Iron Works and dogtrot cabin where he left Dyer. Dyer would be the hook he needed to bring in Jim Hagan.

He tied his horse behind the cabin, loosened the saddle girth, and took the saddlebags and the blanket straight to Dyer's hiding place. At the door to the slave pit, he stopped to light a torch made of old rags.

"Dyer, it's Nelson."

"Christ, man, I thought you left me in this pit to die," Dyer said.

Nelson climbed down the steps, "Told you I'd be back."

He stuck the torch in a crack in the wall and tossed the saddlebags full of food to Dyer.

"Before you eat, I need to have a look at your shoulder and change the dressing."

"Go ahead. Don't matter what you do on my shoulder. Going to eat while you work. I'm half starved."

Nelson unwrapped the bandage and poured the red-oak disinfectant into the wound.

"Damn! Shit! that stings like a snake bite."

"I should get you to a doctor."

"Getting me to a doc gonna get me caught and hung. Hagan and his men will be headed south after the ambush. I have to get back and join them."

"At least give your shoulder a day or two to heal. I'll come back and bring your horse the next trip," Nelson said.

"Guess it's as good a place as any to hide."

"I brought plenty of food and water for a couple of days," Nelson said. He wrapped a new bandage tight around Dyer's shoulder.

"You were good back there in that ambush. Shot that Yankee coming up behind us right off his horse. Ride with me when I head south." Dyer tried to hold a loaf of bread with his bad arm and cut it.

"Let me cut that bread," Nelson said.

"I'm gonna to have to do it myself soon,"

"Heading for Arkansas?" Nelson asked. He thought again of the blue uniformed trooper he had shot.

"Got a meetin' up place down there. It's deep in the mountains, near Buffalo River and the hawksbill crag."

"We can talk about my joining up with you when I come back. I'm going up to the cabin, see if I can get a fire started up in the fireplace. Come up if you feel like it."

"I'm staying here for now. Thanks, Nelson."

Nelson closed the steel bars and pulled the boards back in place. He walked toward the cabin and knelt to feel along the rock foundation. His hand came to a large course stone supporting the corner. The stone had fallen from the cart many years ago when he tried to unload it, and pinned his leg to the ground. He pushed with his other foot trying to get free before his dad saw him. He was too late. His dad jerked him up by the arm and dragged his leg out from under the stone. He told his dad he was sorry. That got him the "Sorry ain't a word I want to hear," beatin' of his life.

Nelson pulled the latchstring on the door and went in the dark cabin to kneel by the fireplace hearth. He found several logs and sticks left by some traveler on the edge of the hearth and stacked them to burn.

When the fire finally flickered to life, he sat, facing the dancing flames. The rustle of crushing leaves behind him caught him off guard. He spun with the .44 cocked in his hand.

"Don't shoot, mister. Lordy', don't shoot no poor nigger man that don't mean you no harm."

"I didn't see you there against the wall," said Nelson, lowering the hammer on the pistol.

"I best go on my way," the man said.

"Chill's on the night. Warm up a bit first," Nelson said, moving to the side to give the man a place in front of the fire.

The man crawled from his bed of leaves across the heavy oak plank floor and found a place to sit facing the fire, far to the edge of the hearth.

In the firelight Nelson watched the man's gnarled hands open toward the warmth of the fire. The gray in his hair extended down his sideburns and frosted the edges of his beard. Twice the man ran his knuckle over a long scar that crossed his cheek and disappeared under the beard.

"That scar. Come from the war?" Nelson asked.

"Comes long before that. I runs away. Dogs caught up to me in the slough, up by the big river. I was took back all dog bit and chewed up."

Nelson noticed the fire had burned to bits of glowing charcoal and stood to look for more logs.

"I'll get some wood, sir," the man said.

The man straightened and went to the back wall of the cabin room. Nelson heard him brush away the leaves that made up his bed and watched him limp back carrying two old boards and a small log.

"How'd you happen to find this cabin?" Nelson asked.

"On the way somewheres else, I 'spect. I'se ain't no run away."

"Never thought you were, all slaves are freedmen now," Nelson said, stocking the fire with a broken stick.

"Old nigger man at the Iron Works told about the child girl slave that lived in this here cabin. Hung her right out there to that tree in front he told me."

"Not here. Over in the town is where they hanged her."

"All I know is, feel the spirits when I'se come here."

Nelson wanted to tell the Negro he felt the same spirits, spending the night in his old cabin. He wanted to ask the man about his missing saddlebags first. The man who had found his saddlebags walked with a limp.

"It was a bad flood came through here. I lost my horse right out from under me."

"Saw them horses, cows and goats all dead on the ground," the man said.

"Did you see a roan horse with a saddle still on?"

"Yes, sir. I seen that horse."

"Were the saddlebags there?" Nelson asked, still looking at the fireplace.

"Yes, sir. Carried them up to the ironworks. I didn't steal nothing, that horse was dead."

"I know. I saw your footprints along the river. Lost your track on the road."

"I don't have those saddlebags no more. Man working at the iron place said he would give me fifty cents for them saddlebags. Never had that much money before."

"Would you know him if you saw him again?" Nelson asked.

"Yes, sir I knows him. He work on them mules and horses right as you get to the iron place."

Nelson realized the blacksmith at the Iron Works had the wax-covered pardons he had brought from Saint Louis.

As the fire burned down the old man went back to his pile of leaves in the corner, and Nelson stretched out in front of the fireplace. He remembered the cold nights he spent by his dying mother's side, in the same spot. He hoped sleep would come soon.

It was morning when the old man got up and quietly lifted the door latch to leave. He stopped halfway out the door to look back as Nelson turned and sat up. "You knows I looked at them papers was in the saddlebags. Don't know words, but I just look at all the letters, must mean something. Master wouldn't let no slave have learnin'."

"You have helped me to maybe get those papers back," Nelson said. "Would you want to help building back a town?"

"Yes sir, I'd be willing to work, long as no man locks me up no more."

"I'll pay you to help us. Need to know your name before I send you off," reaching to shake the Negro's hand.

"My name is Thomas, sir."

"Thomas, a lot of the town of Steelville has been washed away. We're going to need help to rebuild." Nelson told him how to find Miss Gordon and the barn where he could stay. Nelson took two dollars from his money belt and gave them to Thomas.

"This money will buy food until I can get back to Steelville. Tell Miss Gordon you'll be working for Mr. Nelson."

Nelson stopped at the shed and shouted down at Dyer to let him know he would be back in a day or so with food and another horse. Nelson had decided to join Hagan and his men, he and Dyer would soon head south toward Buffalo River.

Back on his horse, he headed down the long ridge to the ironworks and the blacksmith's forge. It wouldn't be his first meeting with the blacksmith, still he didn't know which side of the war the man supported. He pulled up the bay alongside the mule pen and got off.

"Back again? Not looking for another mule, are you?" the blacksmith asked, setting down his tongs and coming out to meet Nelson.

"Thought you might have something else I'm looking for," said Nelson, adjusting the pocket on his jacket.

"Took me a while to figure out which side you're fighting for, mister," the blacksmith said. "Some say you're from here, but fought for the North. Is that right?"

"Yes, sir."

"With you losing your horse and all in that flood, I was sure you would be coming for something I've got," the blacksmith said. "Got the papers hid inside."

The blacksmith disappeared into the forge building and returned carrying the saddlebags. "Here's your saddlebags, mister."

Nelson took the saddlebags without looking inside and reached into his money belt.

"No, sir. All them papers in there, you get them signed and a lot of folks in these parts will be mighty happy. Won't take no money from you, soldier," the blacksmith said, reaching to shake Nelson's hand.

CHAPTER 11

Spaid had ridden the county as the leader of a militia gang during the war, taking anything he wanted. With the war nearly over and nothing coming in, he harkened back to Senator Saunders, his Steelville friend, planning to run for governor of Missouri.

Saunders had been stealing guns from shipments coming to the state of Missouri, and he had Spaid's men take the guns south to sell to the confederates and the militias. Saunders had given Spaid a hand full of money when he told him to kill Nelson Paintier. Paintier's nosing around and telling people about his father's murder would ruin Saunders' chance of becoming governor.

Spaid was sitting on the back porch of his cabin when one of his riders came back from the mission to kill Paintier. The rider had his gun hand wrapped in a bloody bandage.

"Tell me you found him and he's dead, Jasper," Spaid demanded, walking to the side of the rider's horse.

"We found him," Jasper said.

"Tell me he's dead," Spaid demanded.

"We found him, Spaid. Right there in Steelville like you said he would be."

"He's dead? Right?" Spaid said, slapping Jasper on the boot.

"He shot us both. My boy is in bad shape," Jasper said.

"Told you to kill the bastard. If he ain't dead I don't give a shit about your boy."

"I'll go . . . back and kill him," Jasper said.

"Back, fuck! Them busted fingers is turning black. You ain't going to have a hand to shoot with no how. Get to Jefferson City and get some of Saunders' men to ride after him. Don't want to see you again till Paintier's dead. Come back and he's not, I'm going to fuckin' shoot you. Understand?"

"Yes, sheriff," Jasper said, turning his horse and heading for the capital city of Missouri.

War got all the good men killed. I'll have to go after Nelson my own self.

CHAPTER 12

Nelson rode east toward Steelville and turned off the trace every few miles into the deep woods along its sides to watch and see if he was being followed. No saw no one.

Ahead he saw a swayback team of horses driven by a man whose wife sat at his side. Two children stood behind them, squeezed between the wagon seat and a load of furniture. A young calf fighting a lead rope followed behind the wagon. Nelson realized the load of furniture was too heavy for the old team.

When he rode up alongside the wagon the man lowered the driving reins and reached under the seat to bring up a rusty single barrel shotgun. The wagon stopped with a squeal from the rear wheel.

"Look, mister," the man said. "I'm tired of trouble. Don't want no more. Move on by and we will get on our way out of this hell hole."

"Just stopped to see if your horses are doing okay with that heavy load. Got a wheel needs greasing bad, on the back," Nelson said.

"Team is old, but all we got," the man said.

"None of my business, but would be better to lighten that load before the wheel falls off."

"That's right, mister. Ain't none of your business."

"He's just trying to help," the wife said, tugging at her husband's shirt sleeve.

"Sorry, mister. My wife is right. Seems like the whole damn place is gone crazy. Can't even talk to folks next door, supposed to be your neighbors, about what you believe in. When you do, next thing you know, you got a dead cow with her throat slit and a calf that's left to bottle feed."

"Lots of hate built up, from this war," Nelson said. "Going to go on even after the war's over."

"Well we won't be here when that happens," the woman said.

"Don't know with which side your feelings lie, but direction you're headed is Kansas. Doesn't make any difference there which side you believe in. If they know you came from Missouri, likely they will kill you."

"Thanks, mister. Going to head on up north to Iowa or such," said the man, snapping the reins on the backs of the two swaybacks, "Hoping this old team can make it up there."

"Give them a rest now and then. They should be okay. Tell the blacksmith at the Iron Works I told you to stop, he'll put some grease on the wheel for you. Good luck," said Nelson, turning and heading again for Steelville.

He had gone a few hundred yards when a freight wagon came around the bend toward him.

"Haw mules, haw you lazy bastards," the muleskinner yelled, cracking a bull whip over the three yoke team of mules.

Nelson rode into the trees lining the trace to escape getting hit by the careening freight wagon, "You crazy sonofabitch," he shouted.

When the dust settled, he rode back on the trace. The loud crash he heard came from the direction of the freight wagon and team. His first thoughts were of the family he passed and their safety. He spurred his horse toward the crash.

"Goddam-settlers, taking up all the road," yelled the muleskinner, climbing over the side of his overturned wagon.

"Looks like those folks have as much right as you to use this trace," Nelson said, riding around the wreck to check on the bucking mules still hitched to the overturned freight wagon.

"They're dragging that shit spewing calf behind their wagon. Dang lead mules wouldn't run over the darn calf," said the muleskinner, pointing to the bellowing brown and white calf, sliding along behind the wagon load of furniture.

"Maybe this will teach you to not drive those mules so fast. Lead mules seem to be a darn sight smarter than you, skinner," Nelson said, turning back toward Steelville.

"Ain't gonna help me right this wagon, mister?" the muleskinner pleaded, pushing hard to try and get the wagon off its side.

"Reckon not, skinner," Nelson said, leaving the wreck behind. The last two days had worn at him. Being around the dogtrot cabin and the large marble slab that had been placed across the drowned baby's grave sat in his path at every turn. A second slab sat next to the first child's grave. It covered another Mockbee child that had died at five years old. The sorrow he caused that day at the spring pool with the slave girl lasted beyond the war he survived.

The nine-mile ride to Anne's barn gave him time to think about what he would do next. He set his goal long ago to come back to Steelville. Then the Army asked even more of him and he wasn't sure how to go about stopping the guerrilla raids just yet. Darkness would catch up to him before he reached Steelville.

Nelson reined the bay up in front of the barn and swung down. He dropped a stirrup over the saddle horn, loosened the girth and lifted the back of the saddle to let air under it. No need to unsaddle, he would leave before morning, sooner if trouble came.

At the water tank, the horse drank long and hard. Nelson remembered being criticized by the cavalry for letting a horse do that after a long ride, hell with them, horses know what is best when they need a good drink.

He led the bay into the barn, feeling his way along the walls to a back stall.

A hoarse voice commanded. "Drop the reins. Move, and I'll shoot the woman."

"Easy. I'm not moving," Nelson said. "Anne?"

"She got some quick schooling on keeping her mouth shut," the voice said.

"Let the woman go," Nelson said, gripping his pistol.

"What do you want with us?" Anne demanded.

"Shut up, teacher. Lead the horse back out the barn door Paintier. Don't try nothing. The woman is right in front of me."

Nelson had no choice. He turned the bay and walked to the front of the barn and into the moonlight. The man followed with Anne in front to shield him.

"Take your pistol belt off. I want to hear it hit the ground. Then the rifle, on the ground beside the belt."

Nelson did as he was told.

"Woman's walking toward you now. She's riding behind you."

"My saddle's loose, just taking up on the girth," Nelson said. Anne moved to his side and gripped his arm with both her hands.

Anne whispered, "I'm sorry. He surprised me when I came to see if you were back."

"Shut up and stand there," the man said backing in the barn to get his horse. "Both you, get on that horse."

Nelson gripped the stirrup, stepped into it and swung up on the bay. Anne couldn't reach the stirrup; so Nelson easily lifted her by both arms until she could. She sat behind the saddle with both arms wrapped tightly around his waist. Her fingers pinched Nelson's slim belly. Not a time to enjoy her touch.

"It'll be okay. I don't think he plans to kill us," Nelson lied.

"Turn east at the top of the ridge," said the man, riding close behind them, and urging them into a fast walk.

"Where's the boy?" whispered Nelson.

"Asleep at the house. He doesn't know I left," she said.

They had gone less than two miles when the man said, "Stop here. We're going to walk on in. Anything funny and I'll shoot the woman first." Nelson didn't need to be reminded.

The man pointed out a narrow path for them to follow. The path led to a cabin on a steep hillside about a half mile off the trace. Nelson and Anne dismounted in front of the cabin and waited.

"Tie the horse to the rail," said the man. He dismounted and stepped on the cabin's porch.

A voice came from the side of the cabin, "Don't really think you can ride up here without me knowing it, do you, Pa? Keep them out there, I'll get a lamp lit inside."

Moments later the door opened and their captor shoved them through it into the lighted room. He motioned with his rifle to a post.

"Tie 'em up, boy," he said. "Bitch nearly bit my finger off when I grabbed her back there in Steelville."

"Too bad I didn't get the job done," Anne said. "Who lives here?"

"Does it look like somebody lives here? Empty room and all," said the man wearing a vest and long black coat.

"Why us, mister?" Nelson asked.

"Don't remember me do you, boy?" asked the man with the vest. "You're Paintier's nigger loving kid, ain't you?"

"Why the lady? Let her go, you got me."

"Not now, they can't. I've seen them both before. They worked over at the Iron Works until they got fired and ran off," Anne whispered. "Name is Waldron, other one's his boy."

"Want you to know, Paintier. Mockbees were my friends. Don't ride by that cabin without thinking about carrying their dead baby girl up from the spring," said Waldron. "How you went crying and bellyaching to the sheriff that she didn't do it. She did it, she drowned the baby. I stripped her and beat her black ass till she said she did it. Ain't forgot, Paintier. Now they're saying you're a turncoat. Fought for the butcher, Grant. He killed my other boy."

"War's nearly over, mister," Nelson said.

"Well, maybe you and this teacher you've been bedding down going to think different," said Waldron. "Check them ropes, son. Then pull them burning coals out of the fireplace onto the floor. We're leaving them to burn."

Nelson and Anne watched the cabin door slam shut and heard the sounds of the men's horses clatter up the path they had come down. The hot coals the men spread had the wooden floor ablaze.

"Sorry I got you messed up in this, Anne." Nelson tugged at the ropes that held them. The flames slowly spread across the floor toward their feet.

"It was my fault, for going up to the barn in the dark of night looking for you," Anne said.

"I remember that old man. He worked for Sheriff Spaid when I was a boy," Nelson said, trying to work his arm out of the ropes. "Saw him tie the slave girl to a tree and beat her raw, trying to get her to confess."

"Nelson, the fire is getting close to my feet," Anne choked on the smoke.

"Nelson? Aunt Anne?" came the voice from outside the window.

"Joshua, we're tied to a post in here, hurry," Nelson said, fighting to kick the fire away.

It took only seconds for the boy to get through the door and circle around the flames to reach them. Joshua, opened his pocketknife and cut Anne's ropes first.

"How, Joshua? How did you find us?" Anne asked.

"I saw the man take you off. Ran behind following on the trace, but couldn't keep up. Then I saw the mare coming empty. Rode her till I saw the fire."

"Saved us, Joshua," Nelson said, following Anne and Joshua through the open door.

"Found your pistol on the ground, would have shot them if they were still here," said Joshua. "Reckon this makes us kind of even, don't it?"

"Reckon it does. You two ride the bay, I'll walk along side, back to the barn," Nelson said. "Oh, and maybe you better give me that pistol."

They were less than a half mile from Steelville when Nelson saw another fire light up the night sky.

"They're burning my house," screamed Anne.

"Joshua, slide off the horse. Anne and I need to get to her house fast!" Nelson said.

The short ride brought them to the front of Anne's burning house. Smoke poured out of the broken front windows, and the flames surged from floor to ceiling in both rooms. They had gotten there too late to save anything she owned. Out of breath, Joshua ran down the hill to join them.

"Why'd they do this?" he asked.

"Probably trying to burn my diary and manuscript about Steelville," Nelson said. "Something more than just Sheriff Spaid's revenge on me is going on here."

"It's not your fault, Nelson," Anne added, turning away from her burning home. "It was only a matter of time until someone burnt it because of my sister's husband riding with the raiders. Will it be safe for either of us in Steelville now?"

"Is there someplace, someone Joshua can stay with?" Nelson asked.

"Yes, the Olivers," Anne said. "He'll be safe with them."

"You and I need to ride out of here and pick up Dyer on the way," Nelson said, wondering if he was making the right decision in taking Anne with him.

"Are you sure I need to leave?" Anne asked.

"They'll be back looking for you when they figure out you're alive. You know who they are, Anne. Can you get two other horses?"

"I'll get them. Come on, Joshua. I'll take you to the Olivers."

"Hurry, Anne," Nelson said.

CHAPTER 13

Only smoking embers of Anne's house remained when she returned, in a borrowed riding skirt, a white blouse and a short leather coat. She led two more horses, saddled and ready to ride.

"Joshua wanted to go with us, Nelson," Anne said. "I hope he doesn't follow this time."

"Lucky he did last time," Nelson said, taking Anne's arm and giving her a small boost up into the saddle before handing her the lead rope for Dyer's horse. Turning, he clucked to the bay to move off, running two steps alongside before swinging up into the saddle in one smooth motion. At the top of the hill, they turned west toward the dogtrot cabin where Dyer was hiding.

"Push the horses hard, Anne. We need to be at the cabin before daylight."

The morning light caught the riders loping their horses for the last mile of the ride from Steelville to the ridge just above the Meramec Ironworks.

"Behind the cabin, Anne. We'll tie the horses in the woods to the north," Nelson said. "Dyer's hiding under the smoke house. It's a place where the Mockbees locked their slaves up at night."

With the three horses hidden in the woods, Nelson led the way to the smokehouse, giving a whistle to signal Dyer.

"Dyer," Nelson said, lifting the floorboards and grate covering the pit.

"Someone with you?" Dyer asked.

"It's Anne, Dyer."

"Anne, what the hell are you doing here?"

"Couple of fellows tried to kill us last night. Burned down Anne's house," Nelson said.

"Is Joshua okay?" Dyer asked.

"Yes, he's fine, Dyer. We left him with the Oliver family," Anne said.

"Your boy saved us last night. Men got the drop on me and took us to a deserted cabin about two miles east on the trace," Nelson said. "Tied us up and set the place on fire. Joshua got there in time to cut us loose."

"I'm glad you're both safe," Dyer said.

Nelson and Anne checked Dyer's wound and settled in to tell him the details of earlier that night. Dyer knew old man Waldron, and told Nelson he didn't ride with the guerrilla raiders. Nelson was now sure he was being hunted by someone other than an ex-sheriff with a bone to pick.

"Dyer, can we ride south and join your friends down there?" Nelson asked.

"That may be safer for Anne than staying around Stringtown or Rolla," Dyer said. "I think Hagan will be glad to have us join up with them."

"I'm going to ride over to the ironworks and pick up the supplies we'll need for the next few days," Nelson said. "I'll be back in a couple hours."

Nelson climbed the short steps leaving Dyer and Anne to wait in the slave pit hiding place. He carefully pulled the floorboards over the opening and left the smokehouse. Walking across the clearing alongside the dogtrot cabin, he stopped at the hickory tree where Mary had been tied. He ran his hand over the rough scar in the tree bark carved there years before. "MURDERER." Time still hadn't healed the wound.

He loped the bay down the long hill and didn't slow until he reached the river crossing. The flood had eroded the banks leaving broken and fallen trees stretched all along the shore. The spring-fed river ran clear again and he could see deep ruts where the freight wagons had crossed. He dropped the bay's reins and let the horse pick the path across. The horse stopped at midstream and struck the water several times with its front hoof, finally dropping its head to drink.

The stop midstream gave Nelson a chance to study the two riders headed toward the river from the direction of the ironworks. He nervously touched his rifle and lifted it slightly to be sure it would slip from the scabbard if needed and then settled back in the saddle, to wait.

The riders pulled their horses up before reaching Nelson and touched the brims of their hats in a greeting. Nelson got a quick glimpse of a gold badge on the closest man.

"You fellows from the Iron Works?" Nelson asked. He still rested his hand on the rifle's stock.

"We're lawmen. About the only law, if you don't count the Rolla garrison Union Troops," said the man with the badge. "I'm Sheriff Turner. Bill here is my deputy."

"My name's Nelson Paintier. Glad to meet you fellows."

"Paintier? You the fellow saved the Dyer boy in the flood? Clerk at the Iron Works told us what you did," the sheriff said.

"Found him and his ma on the roof of their house, coming down the river out of Steelville."

"Glad you saved the boy. We're heading over to the county seat. Heard the aunt's house burned last night. See if we can help there," the sheriff said.

"When I came through there folks said the house was empty. Teacher got out just fine. Fire burned so fast it looked like it had been set on purpose," Nelson said. "Hope you catch the guys that did it."

Seeing that he was smack dab in the middle of the most lawless part of Missouri, he felt surprised anyone would claim to be "a lawman."

Nelson nodded to the men and headed for the Iron Work's store.

The store was empty except for the clerk Nelson had met on the day of the flood.

"See you're back again, mister," the clerk said.

"Need to stock up on supplies. There's not much available in Steelville. Most stores got washed away."

"Glad to help you out. By the way, fellows were in here a day or so ago asking where they might find you. Told them I thought you might be staying in Steelville," the clerk said.

"Any idea who they might work for?" Nelson asked.

"I don't, but one of the iron workers said he thought the older man was from Jefferson City. Might work for some of the government folks up there. They acted like someone had told them you were headed back to this part of the country. Sure were straight on their facts."

"Couple of their cohorts found me the other night. Wasn't a very friendly meeting. I almost ended up roasted," Nelson said. "If they come back, how about telling them I'm headed up to Jefferson City to pay their boss a visit."

"After what you did to save the boy, I'll be glad to do that."

Nelson walked around the ironworks grounds the rest of the afternoon. The furnaces had been stoked and glowing hot billets of iron were being flattened on the drop hammers. No one seemed to notice a stranger making a visit.

After he climbed the hill to the cemetery and visited his sister's grave, he walked back down the Stringtown trace and stopped in front of the burnt out cabin where his sister had died. An old negro man passed, nodded and headed slowly up the hill toward the carpenter's shed. Nelson thought he remembered him at work at the shed; the man had been a carpenter and had made the small wooden coffin for his sister. The time had come to head back to the cabin for Dyer and Anne, for they had a long trip ahead of them.

CHAPTER 14

When they left Missouri and crossed into Arkansas, Nelson felt sure they were far enough away from the men who were hunting him for Anne to be safe. The ride had taken them several days, each night they had slept in caves and old barns along the way.

"How's the shoulder doing, Dyer?" Nelson asked.

"Can't move the arm all that much, but feels like I'm getting stronger," Dyer said, lifting his arm a few inches. "There's a friend of Hagan's lives half a day's ride ahead. He always welcomed me and the boys to stay in his hayloft. Should be there before night."

"Hayloft sounds really good after where we've been sleeping," Anne said, rubbing her backside.

Dyer led them across a steep ridge and along a rocky trail that led down into a creek bottom. At the bottom, they followed a small stream out into a wide valley where they picked up a well-traveled dirt road.

Later that day, Dyer pointed to a house and barn sitting on the west side of the valley near the creek. Smoke from a wood fire hung in the still air around the gray clapboard house. The unpainted barn sat to the side of the house, half dug into the hillside. As they got closer Nelson noticed the hayloft's front stood open with a double strand of rope hanging from a pulley at the top. A four-prong hayfork was fastened to one strand of the rope for lifting loose hay into the loft.

"That hay loft has got to be full of hay. It is sure looking good," Anne said.

"Hang back. I'll head in first. Don't want Joe to greet us with some double ought buckshot," Dyer said.

Two coon dogs in the yard started barking at them before Dyer got closer than a quarter mile to the house. They still hadn't let up as he rode through the gate and up to the house. Both dogs were making their stand under the front porch. "Joe! It's Dyer Spencer. Got two other friends with me."

A shotgun stuck through a gun port in the front window was slowly drawn back inside. The cabin door opened a crack to allow a view of the visitor in the front yard. Both coon dogs came out from under the porch and stood watching the approaching riders, sniffing for their scent.

"Reckon it is you, Dyer," Joe said, stepping through the door. The heads of two boys popped around the door jamb behind him to stare at the riders in their yard, "Some of Hagan's men came through last week said you'd been shot fighting the blue coats up on the Rolla Trace."

"They didn't get me this time, Joe," said Dyer.

Joe continued, "Been keeping an eye out for strangers, still got some of those crazy bastards from Kansas seeking revenge over here for what we did to Lawrence. They can't seem to get over the whippin' we gave them in sixty-three."

"Will it be okay if we borrow your hayloft for the night?" Dyer asked, as Nelson and Anne rode up.

"You bet you can. Unsaddle and tie up the horses in the barn. I'll have Martha fix you some grub."

"I'll go in and help your wife," Anne said. Swinging from her horse, she handed the reins to Nelson.

"Martha already been cooking for us four, so I'm sure she can add on a bit for the three of you," Joe said, opening the cabin door for Anne.

"How many of the boys made it out of that fracas up on the trace?" Dyer asked.

"Couple of them got pretty shot up. Said they lost two at the first volley. They counted you being dead too," Joe said.

"Would have been captured or dead if Nelson here hadn't rode me out of there. Saved my boy too."

"He's more that welcome to sit down and eat with us," said Joe, turning to look toward the cabin with a hungry twitch of his eye. "Come on in when you get unsaddled."

Dyer led the way to the stall area at the back of the barn. He tied his horse and the other two, as Nelson dropped the girths and slid the saddles off. The ride had been slow for the last hour so they didn't need to walk the horses to cool them out.

"Joe rode with us till his wife had their second kid. Then he started doing more farming and hog raising to keep food on the table for them," Dyer said. Lifting his straw hat, he ran his hand over his dirty hair. "Be nice to slip into the creek back there, it's down the slope off to the side of the barn."

"Food's on the table, boys," Anne's voice came from the front of the barn.

The thought of food made Dyer forget the bath. Both men joined Anne and headed for the house at a fast walk.

The cast iron kitchen stove had a red glow under the edge of the stoker door. A big skillet filled with fresh cooked sausage with gravy simmered on its top. Joe's wife put a final stir on the gravy and carried the skillet to set it on a round burnt spot in the middle of the table. The gravy and home cured sausage would be more than enough to fill their hungry bellies.

"I just baked a batch of biscuits for Joe and our boys this morning. Sure can do another batch later, so dig in, folks. Help yourself," Martha said. "We got enough. Our boys can eat later. They've gone up in the cabin loft thinking up mischief. Got no school round these parts to keep them out of trouble."

"How old are your boys?" Anne asked.

"Young one is two, other going on ten, ain't he, Martha?" Joe asked.

"Be ten in September."

"Anne was teaching school up in Steelville," Dyer said, choking on the big mouthful he had tried to swallow. "Big flood came and nearly washed the town away."

"You heading south to join up with Hagan and his boys?" Joe asked. "Last I heard they where somewhere down 'round Buffalo River."

"Yes, it wasn't safe round Steelville and the ironworks for any of us," Dyer said.

"Welcome to stay here long as you want, 'fore you move on," said Martha. "Maybe Anne can give our boys some learnin'."

"I'll say hello to them in the morning before we leave," Anne said.

After supper the three guests thanked Joe and his wife and headed for the barn.

"Still warm enough. I'm going to head down to that creek, wash away some dried blood and clean up a bit," Dyer said.

"We'll check on the horses, get them some hay, and head up to the loft," Nelson said.

Anne climbed the board ladder into the loft and pitched down several forks of hay into the stall mangers. Nelson led the horses to the windmill water tank to drink, then led them back into the barn. He looked forward to time alone with Anne in the loft.

"Anne, you know Joe and his wife would be glad for you to stay here with them, till we come back," Nelson said.

"I know," Anne said.

"You don't sound too keen on it."

"I feel safe with you. I'm going on with you and Dyer."

"Safe! So far, I nearly got you burned at the stake. Your home has gone up in flames, and here we are headed to meet up with some of the meanest guerrilla raiders outside of Quantrill and his bunch."

"You have a good reason for being here, Nelson. Let me help all I can," Anne said.

Nelson had flattened out a place to lie in the hay and Anne sat down next to him.

"I don't want anything to happen to Dyer. Joshua needs his dad, it'll be hard enough without his mother," Anne said.

"Dyer tells me most of the men who were riding with him want to quit raiding and get back to their families," Nelson said. "I think that could happen soon."

"And you, Nelson. What do you want?" She had moved close and their hands touched.

Nelson closed his hand over hers and with a gentle pull she was pressed against his side. His other hand slid along her neck under her hair; she turned to face him. The kiss came. Neither knew who moved first. It lasted . . . .

"Really quiet up there. You guys asleep?" Dyer asked starting up the ladder into the loft.

"Nope. Just talking about Joshua. Hoping he's ok," Anne said.

Anne slipped her hand from Nelson's and moved to another area of the hayloft to make a bed for herself. Dyer crossed the loft, climbed high in the loose haystack, and was soon asleep. Nelson thought of the spark when he and Anne kissed. He had worried she might have feelings for Dyer, but that fear had left him. Soon his thoughts faded into dreams. Later, the same nightmares that always lingered would come.

"Nelson, wake up," whispered Anne. "I haven't been asleep and I'm worried about the hounds. They're growling, and I think I heard a horse whinny close by."

"Wake Dyer. I'm going to slip up to the front of the loft," Nelson said. "Maybe those Kansas Jayhawkers came back."

Nelson stood, strapped on the .44 pistol, grabbed the Sharps, and moved to the side of the large hay-loading door at the front of the barn. The pale light from the moon made it hard to make out the danger in front of the house and barn.

"See anything out there?" whispered Dyer. Awake and carrying his rifle.

"Dogs seem to be bothered by something out by the fence," Nelson said.

A flicker of light, and then the light of a torch outlined two men. Another torch was lit from the first, then the two men started across the yard.

"Wait," whispered Dyer. "Might be friendly."

The first torch flew through the air toward the roof of the cabin. The second swung back over a man's head, aimed straight at the open door of the hayloft.

"I've got him," Nelson said. His shot dropped the man on top of the torch. A shotgun blast from the cabin porthole aimed at the other man caught him head high, he fell flat on his back.

All hell broke loose in the barnyard. Four mounted raiders charged, firing at the house.

"They don't know we're up here," Nelson said. "Take them out, Dyer."

Three more were dead on the ground before the last rider turned and headed for the gate. A rifle shot from the other side of the loft door knocked him from his saddle. Nelson and Dyer both turned in surprise to see Anne crank the action on her rifle to reload.

"The fire on the roof. I'm going after it. Holler at Joe, tell him we got the last of them." Nelson leapt onto the hanging hay rope and slid to the ground.

"He knows; he's coming out of the house now with buckets," shouted Dyer. He followed Nelson from the loft. "Anne, make sure those fellows on the ground stay there."

The fire lasted only a few minutes after the buckets of water reached it. Nelson slid down from the house roof, and lifted a lantern to check on the attackers lying on the ground.

"This one's dead. Buckshot took off a lot of his face," Dyer said.

"Got one here still breathing, just a kid. Shot hit him in the gut," Nelson said. "Boy, why are you crazy bastards trying to burn down a farmer's house?"

The wounded boy lay with both hands pressed against the hole in the side of his stomach.

"Wasn't supposed to get shot this way," he said. "Just traveling, raising hell with the damn people that killed my mom and dad in Lawrence."

"Let's get him in the house. See if we can help any," Joe's wife said.

Before anyone could speak, the last shot of the day went straight to the middle of the boy's forehead. "Can't let none of this bunch live, Martha," Dyer said. "Come back with all of Lawrence and kill all of you. Got a place in mind to bury this bunch, Joe?"

"I'll get the team hitched up in the morning, load them up and haul them down the valley about a mile, quicksand bog swallow them up quick," Joe said.

"Might trade out the horse I've been riding for one of theirs," Dyer said, "He's a little gimpy on his right front."

"Gonna' take the rest of the horses over by the White River next week, folks there always looking for good animals and don't care where they come from," Joe said.

Next morning, Dyer and Joe loaded the bodies in the wagon and headed for the quicksand bog. It gave Anne and Nelson a chance to slip away to a deep water hole in the creek Martha had told her about.

"I'm taking you along, sir, but not to watch me," Anne said. "I expect you to stay up here watching the path while I take this soap Martha gave me and get clean."

"Can I at least say I'm disappointed at that order, Miss Anne?"

"You can say it but it won't make any difference," Anne said. "No eyes toward the creek unless you hear me drowning."

Anne finished her bath in the creek without being interrupted. Back on the sandy bank she slipped on a white cotton shirt she had borrowed from Nelson's saddlebags, and took her dirty clothes to wash in the running water. The drops of water falling from her wet hair softened the cotton shirt she was wearing, making it transparent. All of the beauty of the shape and shadows of her firm breasts were waiting for Nelson to see.

"Finished down there yet?" Nelson asked, starting to fidget over the scene he was missing on the sandy bank of the creek.

"You can come down now," Anne said, turning toward him.

His wait had been worth it. He took her hand and pulled her to him, gently moving her wet hair from her lips to kiss them softly and tenderly.

"That's all for now, young man. You stink worse than that horse of yours."

"Must be my turn to jump in that creek."

"Oh really, I might have to sneak just one little peek you know," Anne said.

"Not allowed, too many scars I need to hide," Nelson said.

"Here, rub some of this lye soap on them, should help to soften them up quite a bit, if it doesn't burn the rest of your skin off."

Nelson left his gun belt and pistol at Ann's side, stripped off his pants and shirt, and left his long johns to take off when he got in the water.

The spring-fed creek water felt good, and the strong lye soap peeled off the layers of dirt from his neck and arms. He was afraid to try the soap on his hair so he just ducked under for a minute and scrubbed hard. With the long johns off, he gave them a once over with the lye soap and then wrung the water out of them.

"Coming out now," he said.

"Not before you toss me those long johns. You don't really think that little washing got them clean, do you?"

Nelson tossed the underwear to Anne and stayed in the water to watch her give them a second and third scrub down before she hung them over a bush beside the creek.

"Not going to give them back?" Nelson asked.

"Oh, I thought after the look and kiss the white shirt got me, maybe it would be my turn to stare," Anne said.

He paused a moment and then waded slowly from the waist deep water to Anne. She let the white cotton shirt slip from her shoulders and fall to the wet sand. She pulled him down onto her, onto the white cotton shirt below.

Later they sat pressed against each other, the shirt hung loosely over Anne's shoulders. They talked of the fire and how Joshua had saved them. She gripped his arm tightly when he spoke of her home burning. Tears crossed her cheeks; Nelson could tell she had fought to keep them back.

"I would like to rebuild the house for us," Nelson said.

"Come on, time to get the sand off," Anne said with a slight gasp, pulling him behind her into the cold water.

On the walk back up the path to the barn, Anne asked, "Where is Dyer taking us? Do you know?"

"Dyer tells me we aren't far from the Big Buffalo River Valley. There've been a lot of Federal troops pushing down into that area. They caught a bunch of locals mining saltpeter from a cave, making gun power for the Confederates. Shot them all dead on the spot. We will have to be careful down there."

"I know the valley. My folks thought about homesteading there when we first came west. All the good bottomland was settled; nothing left but patches of land up on the benches of the mountains. Daddy took us back north."

"Dyer's been saying we would find Hagan up around an area he calls the hawksbill, big rock ledge sticking out over the valley. Their camp's in the deep woods just before the cliffs, with escape routes off in two different directions," Nelson said. "Take us about two more days to get there."

"Any idea what you're going to do when we get there?" Anne asked.

"How about staying alive, to start with."

CHAPTER 15

"Stay alert, I saw a reflection from something up on the edge of the woods," Nelson said.

"The camp should be just over that ridge. They'll recognize me, so stay close," said Dyer.

"They know we're coming, lookout has a rifle leveled on us," Nelson said.

"Hey, Dyer. Thought you was killed," shouted the lookout.

"Yankees tried hard. Fellow riding with me had a lot to do with keeping me alive," Dyer said.

"Ride on in, Hagan will be glad to see you're alive, Dyer," the lookout said.

When they crossed the ridge into the camp, Nelson picked out the leader from a line of seven men headed for them. He had three men on each side of him and they stood ready for a fight. Each of the men carried two or more revolvers, some holstered, others stuck in their belt.

"Dyer, what the hell do you mean bringing strangers to this camp?" Hagan asked. Hands moved with the word "strangers" to rest on their pistol grips.

"Woman's my wife's sister. Other one saved me from the goddam Yankees," Dyer said. "Shot one clean off his horse as he tried to kill me."

"If I find out you're dragging shit in here it'll get you and them both killed," Hagan said. "Get down; I'll have to find out more about that Yankee killer later."

"Thanks, boss. Bluecoat shot me in the shoulder 'fore he went down," Dyer said, swinging slowly down from his mount.

"Thought you looked tuckered. The girls been riding with us got some coffee brewin'," Hagan said.

The three joined Hagan on the log benches around the camp fire. Waiting for the coffee gave Dyer time to tell him about the flash flood that hit Steelville and how Nelson saved his boy.

"Know about floods on that river, got some family livin' 'bout five miles downstream from Steelville," Hagan said. "They got flooded out of the valley once before, moved their cabin up the ridge case it happened again."

"We had a bad flood there after my dad moved us to the Iron Works," Nelson said.

"Notice you walking with a limp, Nelson. Some Yankee get a shot into you?" Hagan asked.

"Nope, horse went down, took two hits to her chest. Stopped cold in her tracks. I went over the top. Hurt my leg." He wasn't ready to tell which side had shot the horse.

"If you shot a Yankee trooper to save this old sidekick of mine, that makes you good enough to ride along with us," Hagan said. "Coffee up, then get unsaddled. Horses look tired."

Nelson and Dyer unsaddled the three horses and tied them to the camp's picket line.

"Thanks for speaking up for me, Dyer. These boys got mighty fast hands when it comes to going for their guns," Nelson said.

"Wait till you see them really pissed. Break out their black flag, up front of the riders. They'll follow the flag into the gates of hell."

When they returned, Anne sat waiting at the campfire circle. Dyer told Anne and Nelson the camp sat only a few hundred feet from the hawksbill crag. Both wanted to see it, so Dyer led the way to the bluff.

"Walk careful, along here. Lots of loose rock ahead," Dyer said.

"Look at that, Anne," Nelson said, pointing toward the huge ledge sticking out over the Buffalo River valley.

The three of them walked halfway out on the ledge and stood looking at the valley, and river far below.

"Would hate to fall off here," Anne said.

Dyer pointed to the end of the cliff, "Legend tells of a preacher who stood out near the edge of it every day. Lifted his arms to the sky and shouted his prayers to God. On a stormy Sunday morning, a lightning bolt hit the preacher. Lightning so strong, no one found any of his remains. He was just gone. The congregation argued for weeks, some said the devil, others said God took the mean old bastard. A scary place."

"Heard rumors that bushwhackers had thrown men off the hawksbill," Nelson said.

"More than a rumor," Dyer said.

A cold wind blew across the raiders and their new recruits that night.

"Don't think you're going to get all that bed of pine needles do you, Captain?" Anne moved in tight against Nelson's back, pushing for even more room.

"Hope those arguments going on across the camp aren't going to keep you awake," said Nelson.

"What's going on with the men?" asked Anne.

"Men are playing poker to see who is next with the girls," said Nelson.

"Guess I'm lucky you've got the best poker hand in our game, Captain," said Anne.

Back to back didn't last long. Nelson turned toward Anne first.

"You know, lady, my heart glows warmer each day you're with me."

Anne turned to face him, her arm felt for him and pulled him close. Her deep kiss drove away the cold of the night and erased his memories of the war that haunted him day and night. Near morning Nelson awoke to feel the warmth of Anne's breath as it touched the side of his face.

"Only you, no other has ever made me feel this way," Nelson whispered in her ear. She awoke at the sound of his voice and kissed him again and again.

The sun came up fast on the mountain top and found Hagan and his men packed to ride. Dyer had their horses saddled and ready when Nelson and Anne joined him. By noon they were ten miles north of the Buffalo River and hungry.

"Smell coming in on the afternoon wind," Red said. He was Hagan's top side kick.

"Right off fresh hams and side meat that's being smoked, I reckon. It's making my mouth water," Jim Hagan said.

"I feel hungry, like an old hound that's been too long on the trail without even a bone," Red said. "Smell coming from close by."

"Too bad they didn't name you Red Bone after the hound dog. You can smell meat cooking a mile away," Dyer said.

"Gather the boys around, Red," Hagan said, lifting one of his revolvers and checking the loads. "Nelson, you and that .44 ride up here with me. Dyer, you hang back and give the shoulder a rest."

"Circle up, men, over here!" yelled Red.

"Them Yankee troops have pushed us as far south as I'm going," Hagan said to his twelve men. "We got to get some provisions before we split up for good. Smell of the smoking hog meat drawing hard on me."

"Need two of you, get up there. Scout out the place Hagan said. Two of the men pivoted their horses and we gone before he had finished speaking.

"Give them five minutes and we'll follow," Hagan sai

"Sounds like you're splitting up and heading on south after this?" Nelson asked.

"Got folks on down in Texas," Hagan said. "My boy went down there when I made him leave. The fighting was getting real bad up here. Ain't seen him in quite a while."

"Them wanted posters were popping up all around town on us 'fore we came down here," Red said. "No place left for us to go."

"I doubt if I can ever settle again," Hagan said. "Too many people know my face. Let's close up on the boys."

"They're heading back, riding fast," Red said.

One of the riders pulled up in front of Hagan, "Might not want to ride in there, Jim. String of blue coats got the man stretched out by his neck. He's pulled up to the hayloft. Woman screaming somewhere back in the barn."

"How many blue coats?" Hagan demanded.

"No more than a dozen. Some drinking the man's shine," said the rider.

"They're for sure going to kill that man. Do worse with the woman," Red said.

"I know. Then go tell the county that Hagan's boys did it. Maybe we can head that off before it happens."

Hagan and his men tied their horses just over a ridge from the barn and crept forward.

"Sounds like a bunch of them's got the woman in the barn. Red, you and Nelson see if you can get in the back of the barn. We'll get the drop on the ones in the yard."

Nelson and Red got to the back door of the barn without being noticed. Nelson went in first. Red followed close behind Nelson. The woman's screams had been choked into whimpers.

Two of the three Yankees, in the barn, held the woman's legs to the ground, her dress had been ripped apart and twisted around her neck. The third man stood between her legs, his blue pants dropped to his feet, his penis still dripped from the rape he had just committed.

Nelson's first shot blew away the soldier's manhood. The second went straight through his heart. Red fired twice; both of the soldiers that had headed for the door fell dead in their tracks.

Nelson went to the crying woman, and covered her with what was left of her dress and his jacket. He lifted her in his arms and carried her through the barn door.

"She's alive. Them blue bellies inside ain't," Red shouted.

The eight Yankees in the yard had been caught off guard, drunk or asleep. Hagan had them sitting in a row with their hands pulled hard and tied behind their backs. Only one of them had on a full uniform.

"What are you men doing this far south, riding without an officer?" Hagan asked, kicking the closest one in the back.

"They sent us out on patrol. Sergeant got us lost," said the soldier twisting from the pain of Hagan's kick. "We ran out of food."

"Ran out of luck too. They're deserters," Nelson added.

Hagan slammed the captured soldier's head with his pistol side, "Didn't ask for a fucking lie, shit brains."

Hagan's men had cut the barn ropes and lowered the strung up man to the ground. He fell to the ground unable to stand, with his hands on his throat, unable to make a sound from his damaged windpipe. Anne went to the wife and pulled her close to comfort her.

"Damn, Hagan, Nelson's .44 took the raping bastard's dick and balls clean off in there. Then he shot him in the heart as he was looking to see where his parts had gone," Red said.

"I would have let him stand there for a bit to think about what he was missing," Hagan said.

"What we goin' to do with prisoners?" Red asked.

"Think about ways to kill them in the morning. Need to get you boys fed, so we can think on that."

Hagan's men were quick to raid the farmer's smoke house to get meat for cooking on the fire they started in the barnyard. Several of the men searched the farmer's house for anything else they could cook to eat.

Nelson took a plate of fresh cooked bacon and grits to Anne, and joined her beside the empty barn.

"I feel like I'm still in a dangerous place with Hagan. It may have helped to take down those deserters," Nelson said.

"I heard some of his men talking about wanting to go home," Anne said.

"That's about the only thing I have going for me. Probably going to kill me if he finds out I fought for the North."

"Is Hagan going to stay here tonight?" she asked.

"Believe he's going to. Afraid it's going to be a sleepless night for me, sitting with my back to this barn," Nelson said, wrapping a blanket around Anne's back and having her slide her head and shoulders into his lap.

Nelson was still awake when the rider came in a little after midnight. Hagan's guards were the first to meet the man.

"Been looking for Hagan and you boys for over a week now," said the rider. "Have some news he ain't gonna want to hear."

Hagan came out of the farmhouse and hurried to the rider. "You look worried, something you don't want to tell me? Spit it out, damn it."

"It's about your boy," said the rider. "Yankees caught him and the others up east of Jefferson City. Killed most all except him. Like skinning a buck deer, beat the hide right off his back, put him on a horse with a note saying they would do the same to any bushwhacker they caught from now on. Horse carrying him came into Stringtown. He only lasted a few days."

Hagan grabbed the rider by the shirt. "Who? What troops did this to my boy?" Hagan demanded, pushing the rider against the wall.

"One of our men got away; he said it was the officer that cut up your son. Company pendant looked like they were from the Rolla command," the rider squeaked. Hagan relaxed his grip, and eased him off the wall.

"Get everybody up. We're going to drag those fucking blue bellies to the hawksbill and throw them to hell. Goin' to find that sonofabitch that skinned my boy. He'll think hell fire and brimstone been poured all over him when I get through."

With the captured deserters roped together, Hagan and his troops headed to the camp near the sheer cliffs of the hawksbill crag. Several of the captured men in the rope line kept slowing the group down.

"Cut them out," Hagan yelled. "Tie a rope round their waist. Going to drag them behind my horse."

Seeing the two men being dragged behind Hagan's horse did a lot to speed up the rest of the prisoners.

At the hawksbill camp standing over one of the bound up Yankees, Hagan taunted the prisoners, "What's your name?"

"Johnny Brant," the man said.

"Well, Johnny, too bad for you you're not a Johnny Reb. Where would your home be?" quizzed Hagan.

"Wisconsin."

"Wisconsin. Folks in Wisconsin be proud of you? Deserter! Your momma going to miss you? She won't ever know what happened to you," Hagan said.

"What you mean?"

"Mean? Mean today I'm going to throw you off the highest place around here. That's what I mean, you bluecoat bastard," Hagan said.

"Can't, we're prisoners of war," Johnny Brant said.

"Can't! Don't tell *me* can't," Hagan said, drawing his knife from his belt and cutting the man's ropes. "Stand up, I'm giving you a chance. Run for it!"

The prisoner's knees buckled twice before they could hold him erect. He glanced around the camp for a way to run.

"Run that way, Yank. I'm going to count to ten," Hagan said, pointing to a path up the ridge.

Dyer shook his head and looked at Nelson in disbelief. The prisoners all watched and struggled with their rope ties.

"Now run, Johnny. Run for your life. One . . . two . . . three."

Hagan's count only reached five before he shot the man in the back of the head.

CHAPTER 16

With death so close the morning was sober for all.

"Don't want to see them die this way," Nelson said to Anne.

"Isn't there anything you can do?" Anne asked.

"The whole bunch took turns raping the woman. They need to hang for that."

"Hagan is just crazy mad about the way his son was murdered," Anne said.

He's sitting over there quiet. It's time I talk to him."

"Nelson! Are you sure?" Anne pleaded.

"Stay here when they take the prisoners to the hawksbill. Walk off, down toward the creek we crossed just before we got here. If he takes me too, stay close to Dyer."

"All happening too quick. You come back to me, Nelson Paintier," Anne kept her hold on his hand.

"I've got to tell him now, Anne," Nelson said, pulling away and handing her his pistol and holster. "Weapons won't do any good when he hears what I have to say."

Nelson walked across the camp and stood directly in front of Hagan, "Knew about your boy."

Hagan slowly looked up and in a harsh voice, "Knew?"

"Son-of-a-bitch that did it is named Turner," Nelson said. "Union Army command has him locked up, at Rolla. Going to hang for what he did."

Hagan sprang to his feet with his pistol in his hand, and smashed Nelson in the side of the head. The blow dropped him to his knees. "Get up, you fuck. Who the hell are you? How come you came riding in here with Dyer?"

"Didn't come here to do you harm," Nelson said, as he struggled to get on his feet.

"Goddam tired of living then. Might as well stay down there on your knees, 'cause I'm going to blow most of your head off."

"I came here to try and end the killing. My home used to be in Steelville, just like Dyer's. We might have fought on different sides, right now don't matter. It's time it ends, for both sides," Nelson said.

"Mighty fine speech for a Yankee," Hagan said. "Going to let you watch me push these deserters off the cliff, then you're going to follow them. Red, get some rope and tie him up with the rest of them."

"Heard you say you want to get this war over, Hagan. I'm your chance to do that. Send you and your men all home with a pardon," Nelson said.

"Pardon? Whose pardon?"

"Straight from Washington. Lincoln wants to stop the killing in Missouri."

"You're about to see five more killings, right before I make it six," Hagan said.

"Shoving those men and me over the hawksbill is just going to keep the war going on down here."

"Don't think you understand. Yankee officer skinned my boy. Peeled the hide right off his back and tied him to a horse to die. That bastard's going to pay and you along with him."

"You want the officer that did that to your boy?" Nelson asked.

"Want him? I'm going to ride in to that fort at Rolla and drag his sorry ass out. Burn what's left of the place," Hagan boasted.

"I'll get him for you," Nelson said.

"What?"

"I'll get him. Gonna' lose most your men storming a fort like that. What happens to him after I get him is up to you."

"Hold on with the rope, Red," Hagan said.

"Command will move him to Jefferson Barracks in Saint Louis for court-martial," Nelson said. "With six men in Yankee uniforms, I'll be able to march into the Rolla Fort and get him,"

"Red, tie him up," Hagan said. "Gather up the men out by the hawksbill. Drag those raping bastards with you."

Nelson heard the screams from each of the five men as they were pushed over the edge of the hawksbill. He heard the dull echoes of each body smashing far below. Their bones would spend eternity scattered across a mountain valley. Nelson watched Hagan return, walking up the path toward him, his pistol in his hand.

"We try this and it don't work, goin' to make you sorry as hell, mister," Hagan said, sticking the end of his pistol barrel against Nelson's forehead. "Got the uniforms. What else will you need?"

"I'll draw up a general order for his transfer to Saint Louis," Nelson said. His ropes pinched his arms.

"We'll talk about those pardons, if you live. I have the uniforms stowed away on the way north," Hagan said. "If you don't get that sonofabitch for me, I'm going to hang you! Right after I skin your backside just like they did my boy."

"I'll get him," Nelson said.

"Red, he needs watching till we move out in the morning. Best tell your girlfriend over there goodbye, Nelson. Mess this up, and she's going to be a lot of fun for my boys. Tie him to a tree, Red."

Red yanked Nelson's arms around the tree trunk, tied him fast, and then left to join his men around a newly started fire. Anne walked to Nelson's side.

"I can cut you loose when it gets dark," she said.

"Afraid I got you into the middle of some quicksand, Anne. You heard about Hagan's boy and the man who did it. Only way this is going to play out is for me to grab the bastard from the Rolla stockade."

"What about Dyer? Is he going with you?" Anne asked.

"Don't think so. He's your best hope if I don't get back. I think he'll keep you safe."

"Why'd you come back to Steelville after all that happened to you and your dad years ago?" Anne asked. "Must have a death wish?"

"No death wish. Maybe some guilt. Some revenge against the sheriff and his men for murdering my dad. And then a promise I made to a fourteen year old slave girl the night before they hanged her. I couldn't save her. But I let her know someday the truth would come out. I would make sure of that. Best get some rest, Anne. They will be moving you north in the morning."

"Come back safe," Anne pleaded.

CHAPTER 17

Morning found Nelson alongside Hagan and six of his best men. He had watched Anne and Dyer heading out with the rest of Hagan's men for a hideout in the Ozark Mountains. Dyer gave Nelson his word he would keep Anne safe until he returned.

"Ok, Nelson. It'll be your play when we get to Rolla. Mean time, I'm going to keep you right beside me. Any trouble and I'll shoot you so quick you won't even see it coming," Hagan said.

"Going to take a couple cool heads to ride into that stockade wearing Yankee uniforms," Nelson said.

"One's going to be me," Hagan said.

On fast horses, the group of seven left the hawksbill crag high above Buffalo River and headed north toward Rolla. Hagan set the pace, and pushed the group well into the night before they stopped at the bottom of a bluff. Two of his men tied their horses and went toward what looked like a fallen tree. They lifted some of the branches aside and disappeared into the bluff wall.

"Uniforms are hidden back in that cave," Hagan said.

"Won't be the first time they were used to fool Union troops," Red said.

"What you goin' to tell that post commander when we get in there?" Hagan asked, passing around some jerked beef to Nelson and his men.

"That we've come to move the captive to Saint Louis," Nelson said. "We need to get up there fast before Saint Louis troops come for him."

"You better goddam well hope he's still there, Yankee," Hagan said.

"We're going to look a little rough in those uniforms so we need to ride in there at night," Nelson said.

"Gonna stop and get shaved up 'fore going in," Hagan said.

"I'm going to need to write up a general order for the prisoner's release," Nelson said.

"Got paper and ink in my saddle bag. Do that when we stop," Hagan said.

After a couple of detours to avoid known Union outposts, they pulled up the horses three miles south of the Rolla Fort and put on the Yankee uniforms.

Several minutes before midnight, Captain Paintier, with Sergeant Hagan riding beside him, approached the fort's gate. An alert sentry gave the order to stop while they were still twenty yards from the gate.

"Troop couriers, from Saint Louis," Nelson said.

"Advance to the gate, sir," said the guard, turning to call out the fort's guard troop.

"Stay calm, Hagan. No matter what happens in there. We're going to take that sonofabitch out of there before you screw him up, understand?"

"Get on then," Hagan said.

"Open the gate," the guard ordered.

Just inside the gate, the Sergeant of the Guards had six of his troops standing at parade rest when Nelson and Hagan rode up. "Captain, Sir. What brings you to Rolla this time of night?" the Sergeant asked.

"Here to pick up the prisoner Turner. Taking him to Saint Louis for court-martial," Nelson said.

"Came a little late for that, Captain. Troops here was never going to let a hero like him hang for what he did to that murdering shitbag," the Sergeant said. "Didn't take long for him to escape."

Out of the corner of his eye, Nelson caught the motion of Hagan grabbing his pistol. Nelson kicked Hagan's horse in the side and turned into it, forcing the horse toward the still open gate behind them. The guard at the gate leveled his rifle at Hagan a second before Nelson's horse knocked him off his feet. Both of the riders were through the gate and around the corner before the firing started.

Three miles south of the fort, they joined up with the other six men and circled up the horses.

"Troops will be going crazy back there. Won't take them long to come after us," Nelson said.

"I'm going after that sonofabitch. Follow him to Hell," Hagan said. "Saved my life back there, Nelson. I'm going to thank you for that, rather than shoot you."

"Aren't many places he can go, troops from Saint Louis will be looking for him if he goes east," Nelson said.

"He'll go west and find friends with the Jayhawkers in Kansas," Hagan said, "must be at least a day's ride ahead of us by now."

"He'll stay north of Springfield, most likely. Shouldn't be too hard to get a handle on where he's headed in that direction," Nelson said.

"We've got lots of friends around there that will give us a hand tracking him," Hagan said. "Head em up, boys. We're headin' for Kansas."

"Hold on, Hagan. Eight of us riding off in that direction will leave a trail wider than a set of wagon wheels," Nelson said.

"Guess you're right. You're coming with us, Red. Rest of you men lead the Rolla troops off south, set up a running ambush when they least expect it," Hagan said.

CHAPTER 18

Having ridden throughout the night, the three men pulled up their mounts for a rest alongside the Piney River. The horses had started to sweat. Patches of white foam oozed out from under the saddles and around the edges of the bridles. The horses stopped willingly, letting out deep breaths from being winded.

"Doubt if he's pushing this hard to get to Kansas," Hagan said. "Doesn't know the devil himself is on his heels."

"If we guessed right about where he's headed, there's only a couple traces through here for him to take. You thinking the same, Hagan?"

"Yep. He should be only a half a day ahead now," Hagan said, swinging from his saddle. "He'll be stoppin' to bum some food before today is over. Give us a chance to find out if we're on him."

"Till we find his trail for sure what do you think of splitting up on these traces?" Nelson asked.

"Good idea. Screw me up and you know what's going to happen to that pretty schoolteacher been riding with you."

"I know, Hagan. Told you I'd help get this guy and I meant it."

Hagan nodded. "OK, Good place to meet up north of Lead Town on the rail line that runs through there. If you find him holed up somewhere, don't kill him, hear! I'm going to do that slow, make him suffer like my boy did."

"I won't," Nelson said.

"Take the north trace, Nelson. Red, you're ridin' with me."

The north trace Nelson followed crossed deep valleys with steep descents and climbs. He had been walking his horse to give the mare a rest when he came upon a rundown shack alongside the trace. The old man on the porch reached for a crutch before he pushed himself erect in his chair.

"Can I ride up?" Nelson asked.

"Looks like you're comin' anyway," the old man said.

The man's heavy beard and long white hair made him look over sixty at first, but as Nelson got closer he placed him in his thirties. When he let the reins slump, the horse walked the rest of the distance to a hitching post in front of the house and stopped.

"Get down, mister. Sit a bit." the man said, pointing with his crutch to the edge of the porch.

"Name's Paintier. Been sitting out here long?"

"Been out here since they took my leg and sent me home. I still think about killin' all them that was coming at us in that fight."

"Hard to forget, ain't it?"

"Ain't a matter of forgetting, matter is there ain't nothin' else to think about now."

"Been following a Yankee a couple of us want really bad. Think he might have come through here."

"I sit out here most the night. Don't do no good goin' inside and tryin' to sleep. Just end up fightin' all those battles over and over in my head. Least out here the air's fresh and I'm not shut up no more like when the Yankees had me in prison."

"Why'd they take your leg?"

"Yankee doctor cut it off. Said it was rotten anyway and I was going to die if he didn't. Funny thing, first their army tries to kill you, then along comes their doctor and tries to save you. Don't make no damn sense to me."

"War's a crazy thing."

"Rider you're after came through here about dawn. Stopped when he saw me sittin' here. Seen his dirty Yankee uniform, had my shotgun up to shoot him 'fore he took off. Hope you catch him."

"Going to," Nelson said, thanking the man and heading west again. He guessed he would close up the gap before night if Turner stopped for food or to steal a gun.

Paintier saw only a few scattered houses along the trace during the next four hours of riding. For the last quarter mile, the winding road had descended into a deep valley. Nelson heard running water even before he saw the hundred foot wide blue spring flowing from under a bluff and into a narrow stream. A well-kept barn sat on the bank of the stream with a water wheel turning in the current.

A dozen wooden barrels sat in front of the barn, each one with smoke coming out the top. Nelson knew right away the barrels were being seasoned for whiskey. Before he got to the barn the sound of a water driven saw inside stopped. Two rifles were pointed at him from behind stacks of barrel staves in the doorway.

"Easy there," Nelson said. "Looking to stop for a drink of that spring water and anything you keep in those fine barrels."

"Last fella stopped, stole one of our rifles and more than a quart of our whiskey," a woman said.

"Was he wearing a Yankee uniform?" Nelson asked.

"Nope, just a blue shirt and some pants a foot too short for him."

"Sounds like the fellow I'm chasing got a change of clothes. He's a Yankee that needs killing really bad."

"You're welcome to climb down from that saddle and get that drink. Whiskey gonna' cost you a nickel, Mister. You ain't that far behind him," said the man.

Nelson led his horse to the creek. After the mare drank he went back to the barn for a shot of Ozark whiskey and something to eat. He wasn't disappointed by either.

"If that Yankee drinks much of that quart you'll find him lyin' beside the road somewhere up ahead. Our whiskey will kick him like a mule," the man said.

A half hour later Nelson rode out with a warm feeling in his gut not only from the whiskey but also knowing he was pushing the escaped Yankee to a meeting with his maker. The light from the full moon helped him keep riding through the night.

CHAPTER 19

Once he rode out of the steep valley country of the Ozark Mountains, the trace settled onto level ground. Here the virgin timber crowded each side of the narrow pathway and made ambush possible from either side. He wished Hagan and his men were there leading the way with their black flag flying, throwing fear into all who saw the *flag of give no quarter*. Turner could be waiting ten feet to the side and out of sight. Nelson spurred the horse into a run.

After two stops to give the horse a rest, he rode into a settlement of half a dozen houses and a store. Tying up to the hitching post in front of the store he climbed over the two broken steps and went in.

"Howdy young man," came a man's voice from in the back. "Be up there in a minute."

Nelson looked around the counters, noticing the short supply of food items on the store shelves.

"Not a lot to eat on them shelves, is there?" asked the store clerk.

"Damn fighting is making things hard to get down here, I bet," Nelson said.

"Folks that raise their own food are still hungry. Both sides come raidin' and steal from them and me."

"Name's Nelson. Been traveling for a couple of days looking for a murderin' Yankee."

"Ain't seen nobody much. Only had one fellow stopped in this afternoon, besides you."

"Mind telling me what he looked like?"

"Tall man, wearing a blue shirt," said the storekeeper. "Traded me a quart of good whiskey for an old rusty six shooter I keep here on the counter."

"That's the fellow I'm looking for. How long ago did he leave?"

"He ain't left, as far as I know. Took up with one of our town whores and headed up the street with her about twenty minutes ago. Should be 'bout done. Woman is known for her speed with a man. He's ridin' a dark bay horse, should be easy to find in this little town."

"Thanks mister. Going to have a look for that horse."

The bay horse stood behind the run down shack at the end of the street. A military saddle with an empty scabbard sat on the horse ready for the man in the house to ride. Nelson stood across the street waiting, using his horse for cover. He slid the action on his rifle to chamber a round and backed up alongside a tree.

Nelson saw the curtains move and then the front window of the shack shattered. The shot from the house hit Nelson's mare in the front leg. The wounded animal reared and stumbled, knocking Nelson and his rifle to the ground. He got up firing his .44 at Turner on his horse, headed down the street. Nelson ducked when shots came from the door of the house.

"God damn it, lady." Nelson yelled. "Quit shooting at somebody you don't even know."

"Ain't shootin' at you, mister. Just the runoff bastard that didn't pay me nothin' for my pussy," said the woman at the door.

"Too bad you didn't hit him. The sonofabitch shot my horse. Just up and shot my damn horse."

The woman had stopped firing at Turner and stood in the doorway naked as the day she was born.

"Why don't you come on in here and finish off what that prickless bastard started."

"Lady, best you get on back in that house. I've got to shoot this mare and I ain't happy about it at all," Nelson said. Looking at the mare's shattered leg, before he walked in front of the shivering horse to put her down with a big .44 slug to the head.

"Damn it to hell anyway," Nelson said kneeling beside the mare and feeling for any heartbeat.

"Any idea where I can get another horse?" Nelson asked the woman still watching from her door.

"See the man at the store. Keeps a couple horses at a farm just up the road," the woman said. "Fix you right up. Sure you don't—"

"Hell no!"

More than three hours had gone by before Nelson settled with the storeowner for a sound horse and paid him to take care of the dead mare, up at the end of the street. The soldier Nelson chased knew he was being followed and didn't give a hoot about shooting a man's horse.

An hour out of town Nelson heard a train whistle off to the south. From the direction of the sound, he knew the trace ran parallel to the tracks and the meeting place with Hagan and Red.

"Don't like riding another horse straight into an ambush, boy," Nelson said, talking to his mount. "Tracks look like he's riding full out."

Nelson knew Turner had several more days before he could reach Kansas and the safety of one of the Jayhawker towns. He followed at a steady trot, letting the fleeing prisoner push ahead and wear out his mount.

Another train to the south, closer this time, let Nelson know the trace would soon join the tracks at the meeting place with Hagan. With a bit of luck, Hagan may have caught Turner by now.

An hour later, Nelson rode up a steep bank to the railroad line built along the top of a swell. A short distance west, Hagan surprised him and came from behind a stand of willows to the south of the tracks.

"Didn't have any luck on the south trace. You?" Hagan asked.

"He's not far ahead, now. Had a run-in with him back there a ways. He thought he had enough time to stop for some Ozark pussy. Tried to wait him out. The bastard must have seen me. He shot my horse. Been only a couple hours behind him all day."

"I've only been here 'bout an hour. Didn't see nobody pass," Hagan said.

"Tracks still on the trace. His horse lost one shoe back there a ways," Nelson said shifting in the saddle to look back to the north where he'd been riding.

"Lead on back to the trace, Nelson. It's gettin' too late to corner him tonight."

"He'll need to get another shoe on, riding on all this rock. I've been letting him string out a bit so he wouldn't be sure how close I'm getting. He'll have to find a blacksmith. Horse is startin' to favor that right foot."

"We're close to Lead Town, he'll slip in there for the night," Hagan said, dismounting and taking a hoof pick to each of his horse's feet. "Picked up some shale crossing that track."

"Only one trace out of Lead Town that headed west," Nelson said, following Hagan's example and checking his horse's hooves.

"What you got in mind?" Hagan asked.

"Thinking you might ride hard on past Lead Town and I follow him in there and run him out. Let him start out on the trace. We could have him boxed in, once he's out there a ways," Nelson said, lifting his hat and brushing his hair back from his forehead.

"I want to see his face when he finds Jim Hagan blockin' his path," Hagan said, lifting his pistol from the holster and pushing it back solidly and securely. "I'll be out about ten miles on the other side of Lead Town. What's this bastard ridin'?"

"He's hard to miss wearing a blue shirt, sitting a big dark bay horse. I'll be tight on his ass out of Lead Town. He'll be pushing the bay hard. Watch him, he's not goin' down easy."

"We'll see 'bout that. Take Red with you this time, I want that bastard to myself," Hagan shouted, joining the trace at a gallop.

With no daylight left, Nelson and Red rode into the mining town and left their horses behind a hardware store. They walked around the store and down the wooden plank sidewalk.

"Hagan will be mad as hell if we kill this bastard," Red said.

"Want to try and run him out of town, if we can," Nelson said. "He'll head west on his own."

"Smelled a blacksmith firing up his forge when we were still up the road a bit," Red said.

"He's got that shoe on by now. If we're lucky he'll stop to get something to eat."

They had passed the front of the hardware store when they heard the shots up ahead. They ran toward the noise and saw the powder flash from guns.

"Coming from the balcony, looks like the saloon up ahead," Nelson said.

"Somebody comin', goin' like hell out of here," yelled Red as the rider passed them.

"Hard to see, but it looked like the bay Turner was riding.

Up ahead lanterns were being hung in front of the saloon.

"Come on, Red. We need to find out what went on up there," Nelson ran the rest of the way to the saloon.

"Need a posse over here," shouted a man wearing a badge.

"Anybody get a look at that guy?" Nelson asked stepping into the light of the lanterns.

"Ask the gals upstairs," the sheriff said. "Herded all them whores in one room up the steps there, and took all their money. Them gals catch him, be some serious cuttin' going on."

"You see the horse he rode out on?" Nelson asked. Been chasing a Yankee riding a big bay horse missing a back shoe."

"He came in 'fore dark. Rode the bay down to the smithy to get the shoe on. Came back to the saloon to eat. Took the nigger gal upstairs. Next thing I knew he came rippin' down the steps with the gals all screamin' and lookin' for their pistols to kill the bastard," the sheriff said, taking out his pistol and spinning the cylinder to check his loads. "See which way he headed out of town?"

"Sounded like he rode off to the east," Nelson lied. He didn't want anybody chasing Turner but him when the unlucky bastard rode up on Hagan's ambush.

"Ladies will want me to mount a posse up quick; they worked hard for those earnings he took," said the sheriff with a little snicker.

"Might you have helped on those earnings, sheriff?" Nelson ribbed, turning to go into the saloon to look for something to eat and drink.

"Be welcome to have you boys ride out with us in the mornin', mister," the sheriff said.

"Thanks, Sheriff," Nelson said.

Nelson and Red pushed through the double doors of the saloon and found the way blocked by three women, each wearing nothing but an open robe and each carrying a smoking pistol.

"Bastard got the drop on Molly. Threatened to shoot her if we didn't cough up." This gal stood out, taller and wider than any of the other four.

Walking up to the bar, she picked up a half-empty bottle of whiskey, filled three glasses, and smashed the empty bottle across the edge of the bar. Nelson was surprised she hadn't torn Turner's arms off by herself.

"Did we hit him?" asked a dark skinned girl, looking hopefully at Nelson.

"Don't think so. Rode by me headed out of town fast. He's a hardass Yankee I've been chasing."

"Buy us a drink, sweetheart? We're done bare ass broke, see," said the redhead opening her robe and pushing her bare breasts into Nelson's side. He turned away, reached into his pocket for a coin, and slapped it down on the bar. It would buy several drinks for the girls.

Nelson needed rest. He and Red could pick up the trail in the morning. They would have to look for the tracks of a horse with one new shoe in the daylight.

"Get something to eat, Red. This will take care of that and any other thing you might like," Nelson said, flipping him a coin. "I'm going to rest on the bench out front till first light." Grabbing a small jar of salt pork that sat on the bar, he headed for the swinging doors. He got only a couple bites down before stretching out on the bench and falling asleep. The girls didn't follow; they were getting ready to give Red the ride of his life.

Before dawn Nelson climbed the steps in the saloon looking for Red. He found him sprawled across a double bed draped with womanhood and smelling like he just took a bath in a pig pen.

Back with the horses, Nelson began picking out the dirt and small rocks lodged under their steel shoes. As he finished, Red came around the corner of the hardware store, still tucking in his shirt and buttoning his pants.

"Three women soft as melted butter on the outside, but harder than them steel shoes inside."

"Know what you're saying, Red," Nelson said, packing the half-empty jar of salt pork into his saddlebag. "Let's push that bastard . . . hard. Hagan will be waiting for him west of here."

"Should be light in a few minutes. We'll be able to follow his horse easy with that new shoe," Red said.

It didn't take Red long to find the horse's tracks. Falling in to follow Turner, they settled into a gallop, slowing only to make sure they were still on his tracks.

"Track showing . . . he stopped . . . ," Red said. "He's thinkin' no one is chasin'."

"Must have waited till daylight. Can't be that far ahead now."

"He pulled out quick though, must have heard us coming. Tracks show he's goin' at a hard run now."

"Knows we're back here," Nelson said. "Watch if he slows . . . might try to waylay us." Both men spurred their horses into a run.

CHAPTER 20

The thunder of their running horses drowned out the noise of the gun battle coming toward them from around the next bend. A single rider came first, his horse stretched out in a run, turning to glance behind and waving a pistol in his hand. "It's Hagan," shouted Red, pulling up his horse.

Hagan passed Nelson and Red and slid to a stop. "They're comin' - get ready - about six left, Yankee troops been shootin' at me for the last two miles."

The mounted troops rounded the bend, coming through the dust from Hagan's horse, each one firing blind at the guerrilla they chased. They pulled their horses up at the sight of the new opponents.

Hagan yelled, "Come on, Red. Good place as any to die." Taking his second pistol from his belt, he charged headlong toward the surprised troops. The guerrillas rode with their reins in their mouth and a pistol in each hand, their well-trained horses holding their ears flat on their heads and running headlong into the stunned federal troops. Hagan's first shot took down the lead rider; Red's hit a trooper who fell from the saddle onto the trace. Nelson fired, his shot going over the head of his target.

The four troops that were left turned and slumped low in their saddles as they headed back west.

"Let em' go," Hagan yelled. "They won't stop till they get to Kansas City."

The pause gave Nelson time to think. What in the hell was he doing, riding and helping the guerrilla leader he had been ordered to kill or pardon. He realized that quicksand was closing in all around him. Anne traveling with the rest of Hagan's men, and Hagan meaning to skin the guy they were chasing. Way too many things could go wrong if he didn't help Hagan get Turner.

"Red, find his track. He had to come through here," Hagan said. "Didn't get past me."

"Turner's horse has got a new shoe on the right rear, Hagan," Nelson said. "He had to turn off somewhere close by when he heard the gunfight coming at him."

Nelson rode slowly along the north side of the trace, Red along the south, looking for some sign of where Turner had turned off. Hagan rode picket, watching the trace out in front.

The second time Nelson dismounted to walk up deer paths that crossed the trace, he found the spot about twenty yards up where Turner had stopped and turned his horse, watching the fight back on the trail. Nelson gave a sharp whistle that brought the other riders to his side.

"Came through here . . . headed on north," Nelson said.

"Can't be far ahead." Not pausing, Hagan led the way up the steep climb in front of them. The tracks on the rocky trail were hard to follow, so Hagan motioned for Red to take the lead.

"He can track a coon swimmin' in water," Hagan said. "Been followin' behind that red top of his for four years now. Ain't never let me down on followin' a track."

Hagan pulled his horse up beside Nelson, waiting for Red to pick up the track.

"Told Red if anything happened to me out here to go back with you. Take the pardons and get home. Losin' my boy . . . made me think. Been lucky some Yankee like you ain't shot me."

"Now one is helping you shoot Yankees. Ain't worth even a chuckle, is it?" Nelson said, shaking his head.

"Red's on him again," Hagan said, starting up a steep trail to their right. "There's a river bluff up ahead a ways. We might have him by the balls real soon."

What in the hell makes a man crazy enough to kill like Turner did, wondered Nelson. Had he seen casualties? Men stacked in heaps, wounded men buried in mud, with the fight going on back and forth across their bodies, was that enough? Over a year had passed, and still that place he had fought for Grant, The Wilderness, haunted him. Never had the urge to kill been so strong or savage. They had been animals, not men. Nelson urged his horse on.

The three horses stopped nose to tail. Hagan pointed at two elk, their heads up sniffing the air to the left of them.

"Afraid he's got a lead on us," Hagan said. "Elk wouldn't be just grazin' this close behind him." Both elk broke into a run at the sound of voices, crashing through the timber.

Red dismounted and knelt beside the trail. He picked up a broken chunk of moss. "Moss is still damp on the back. Horse went through here less than an hour ago."

"He's turned the horse loose . . . go'in on foot now," Nelson said. "Elk would've smelled a man."

Hagan caught on quick, "Sonofabitch knew we would track him down on horseback. Never find him in here on foot. Shit."

"Horse will stop to graze . . . I'll make sure," Red said. He left to follow the horse's trail on up the ridge. He came back in less than ten minutes. "Horse is up there . . . bridle . . . saddle both gone."

"Head back. Find where he left the saddle and Red can pick up his track," Hagan said.

CHAPTER 21

A quarter mile down the trail, Red found the saddle. Turner had left the horse's tack covered with leaves and brush so they wouldn't see it right away. Red found Turner's trail in no time.

"Started off west," Red said. "Won't be in a hurry. He knows we can't follow him on horseback through the thick brush."

"I'm going in to find his sorry ass," Hagan said. Climbing off his horse, he handed the reins to Red.

"Rather you get back up there," Red said. "Leave his track to me. I'll push him out somewhere up ahead."

"He's going to come out of there desperate. He'll need water, food, another horse if he loses us," Nelson said.

Hagan took the watch from his pocket and handed it to Red, "Fire a pistol shot every hour so we can tell how far you've tracked him."

After a look to check his pistol's loads, Red disappeared into the brush, leaving his horse to Nelson.

Back on the trace, Nelson and Hagan walked their horses west. Nelson led Red's horse alongside his. The first pistol shot came right on the hour. They could only guess how far west the sound came from. Stopping, they waited for the next hour's shot.

"Bound to be a creek crossing up ahead, we can ride up stream half a mile or so and wait till Red runs him out," Hagan said. He spurred his horse into a lope.

In less than two miles they found a stream crossing the trace. They waded the horses up the streambed, swimming them across deep holes of water. Hagan pointed out a place on the bank for Nelson to wait, then rode on north. In less than an hour, they both heard the next shot. A rifle shot. Nelson rode up the stream to Hagan. Three more shots followed. They were from a pistol.

"Red's in trouble. That's our signal," Hagan said. "Need to get back to where we found his saddle." Both men headed back to the place where Red started tracking Turner. At the start of Turner's trail, "Nelson, stay with the horses. That sonofabitch doubles back, kill him."

Nelson didn't like waiting. Especially not holding three horses and unsure what might come out of the brush. He tied the three mounts on the side of the trail and found a place to watch just off the narrow trail.

The wait seemed forever before Hagan came out of the brush carrying Red over his shoulder. Nelson hurried to help him lay the wounded man on the ground. The front of Red's shirt was stained dark with blood.

"He's hit . . . bad," Hagan said.

"Leave me here, dam it," Red gasped and passed out.

Nelson cut Red's shirt off and ripped it into long strips. "Shot didn't come out," He headed for the jar of salt pork in his saddlebags. "Get this wrapped tight with the pork against the hole. Should be enough to stop the bleeding. Going to sting like hell when he wakes up. "

"Nelson, you're going to have to take him back to Iron Town, closest doctor would be there."

"You know the way Turner's headed he is going straight for Lawrence, Kansas. Don't you?" Nelson said. "They will welcome him like a hero there."

"Lawrence? Shit. Wasn't much of the place left after my last visit with Bill Quantrill."

"If they catch you there they'll do more than hang you," Nelson said. "I'll have a lot better chance of dragging Turner out of there than you."

"I've been putting a lot of trust in a damn Yankee, Nelson, but you do make sense. Best not do me wrong. Still thinkin' about you missin' that trooper back on the trace this mornin'."

"See if we can get Red awake," Nelson said as he ignored Hagan's comment and slapped both of Red's cheeks without any reaction.

"Wake up goddam it, Red. Can't lose my best tracker to some fuckin' murderin' Yankee," Hagan said.

Nelson winced.

"Have to tie him in the saddle," Nelson said. "Wrap a blanket around him."

With Red half awake, they tied him half-sitting onto his horse. Both knew he would die before night if he didn't get to a doctor to remove the bullet and stop the bleeding.

"Gonna get him to a doc, then comin' back out to wait for you," Hagan said.

"Wait along the border. I'll come back along the place the Federals tried to head Quantrill off on his way out of Lawrence."

"Know that place too damn well. Not goin' to ask how you know it, Nelson."

"Something happens . . . I'll drag him back to your Buffalo River den."

Alone again, Nelson planned the next couple of days and his ride to Lawrence. Turner would have to steal a horse soon and then travel through a lot of burned out land before he got out of Missouri. "I'm going to beat you to Lawrence you son-of-a-bitch." With a sense of urgency, he spurred his horse toward the guerrilla-ravaged town of Lawrence, Kansas.

CHAPTER 22

Nelson knew the Lawrence folk would welcome a wounded Yankee officer, so he put on the blue pants from his saddlebags and wrapped a bandage around the leg. More than a couple of days passed while he waited on the porch of Lawrence's only hotel for Turner to show up. Nelson knew the Kansas Jayhawkers would welcome Turner as a hero when they found out what he had done to a bushwhacker.

Turner didn't look much like a hero, when he showed up riding an old skin and bone mule. The mule had patches of black soot all along his side and looked like no one had fed him for months. Nelson knew the mule must have been left to roam on the burned out no man's land along the Missouri-Kansas border.

Turner rode right past the hotel without noticing the man slumped on the bench with a bandaged leg. Nelson's deception had worked. Turner urged the mule up to a hitching post in front of the "Lose It Here" saloon.

"Hope that fellow just passed ain't no Johnny Reb," said the man standing to the side of Nelson's bench.

" 'Spect he ain't," Nelson said. "Hear the good folks of Lawrence would likely offer him lunch and then hang him."

"Lost my wife when they come. I was out tendin' my field. They caught her comin' out of the hardware store . . . they just rode her down. Found her layin' dead in the street," the man said.

"We killed some of the bastards . . . caught them headed back toward Missouri," Nelson said. "Welcome to sit."

"Reckon I can, for a while. My name is Mesman. Yours?"

"Just Captain will be fine. Been fighting for so long almost forgot the rest that goes with it. Yes, just Captain."

"Wife and me, we're Dutch. Came out here from Pennsylvania back in fifty-six. Never thought much about slaves and such. Came through Missouri on a steamboat."

"Think a lot of the folks came here the same way. They saw how the slaves were treated along the Missouri River towns. Got their temper up, some took to raiding back in southern Missouri."

"Never done none of that. Back in Pennsylvania some of us Dutch got treated bad. Came out here to get away from it. Sorry now I ever come."

"Lucky in some ways you didn't stay in Pennsylvania. Fighting there wasted away a lot of the state, and the people just trying to get out of the way of the war," Nelson said, watching as a unit of federal cavalry passed the hotel.

Nelson made an excuse and left Mr. Mesman sitting on the hotel porch. He needed to find another horse before nightfall. No way would he take Turner back to Missouri on a worn out mule.

Before that, he made a stop at the saloon to check on Turner. Turner wouldn't remember him, he hadn't been close by when Turner get chewed out by another officer months ago in Missouri. Nelson found him in the back of the saloon surrounded by half a dozen Lawrence, Kansas Jayhawkers who were buying him drinks and listening to him telling about killing some of Bloody Bill Anderson's boys in Missouri.

Hell, he won't even know when I carry him out of there tonight. Now for a horse.

He left the saloon and walked on up the street toward the stable sign just ahead.

"Howdy, mister. You look mighty sore to be walking," said the stable owner.

"You could be right, sir. Need a sound horse."

"Most horses out there in my corral are work horses. Cavalry buys up all the rest. Too many of their horses get shot. Got mules in the back. Have to take both mules. One won't go without the other."

"Rather have a buffalo than another mule."

"Am keepin' a big mustang for my brother. Brother's afraid of his spirit. Big roan horse. Wants fifty dollars for him. Take him; ride him out before you decide."

The thought of a roan with spirit cheered Nelson. He had wanted another horse that would fit his riding, another like Blue. Always willing to climb the rock shelf, claw up, and get him safely to the top.

"Let's saddle him up. Think my leg can stand a little spirit from a horse," Nelson said.

The mustang sniffed hard when they approached his stall. His ears lay flat against his head.

"Somebody been treating this guy mean?" Nelson asked. He picked up a lead rope from the rack.

"My brother ain't easy with horses. Never had no business with a stallion. So we had him cut a while back. He still got plenty of fire in him," said the stable owner. "Took a chain to him coupla times. Last time the horse got out of the stall it chased my brother clean out of the barn."

"Just set out the saddle for me. I'll get to know this fella alone," Nelson said, opening the stall door, watching, as the horse backed to the far corner facing him with ears still flat.

"Easy fella . . . not going to hurt you," whispered Nelson, walking slowly toward the side of the mustang's head. "That'a boy, get my smell," sliding the lead along the outside of the horse's neck and stroking his front shoulder. The ears came up a bit, one turned toward the new man at his side. Nelson attached the lead to the horse's halter and rubbed his hand along both the horse's sides before leading him into the barn's aisle.

"Ain't seen nobody with courage enough to do that for awhile," said the stable owner. "Not after he stomped my brother's dog to death. Named him Killer right after that."

"Anything else you want to tell me now, before I ride Killer?" Nelson walked around the horse, lifted his feet and tapped the center of each hoof to check for soreness. The horse didn't flinch. He took a curry brush to the gelding's sides and croup before saddling, then led him to the street before mounting the fifteen hands tall animal.

"Easy, just a walk for now." Always talking to the horse. Nelson could feel him loosen up and relax. Someone had done a good job breaking the mustang. The horse flexed on command, bending each direction, and then changing leads without queues into figure eights. He rode at a full gallop and then half a mile from town slowed before he reined the horse down into a deep ditch. The mustang climbed out with the power and agility Nelson had always looked for in a mount.

Back at the stable, Nelson flipped the owner two twenty-dollar gold pieces. "Need the saddle and bridle too." He waited for the answer.

"Reckon I'm a lot happier to get that horse out of my brother's hands than you might be to get him," the stable owner said.

Back at the hotel stable, Nelson loosened the horse's girth and walked the fine animal for a few minutes to cool him out from the workout. He tied him and asked the stable keeper to saddle his other horse and keep them both ready to ride.

Nelson paced his room and finally went down to the hotel dining room and ordered the first steak he had eaten since the war started. He drank a cup of strong coffee before leaving his room key at the desk and going to be sure the horses were ready. When he passed the saloon he saw Turner had passed out in a chair near the front of the drinking establishment.

At closing time for the saloon, Nelson entered, telling the bartender he was looking for his friend. The bartender pointed him out in the corner and offered his help to get him out.

"Come on buddy - stand up. I'm taking you to your room," Nelson said, getting Turner to his feet and guiding him out the door. Turner could barely walk, but Nelson managed to get him out of the tavern and around to the back of the hotel.

"Where . . . we . . . goin?" Turner sputtered, leaning against the saddle.

Nelson grabbed Turner's belt and hoisted him flat across the saddle. "There, go on back to sleep." With only a couple of moans coming from the drunk, Nelson had him tied across the saddle and covered with a blanket. Climbing on the mustang, Nelson led the horse and his captive toward the border. "We'll have him back in Missouri by morning, Killer," Nelson said, talking to his new horse. Gonna have to change that name, he thought.

CHAPTER 23

"Get me the hell out of this," mumbled Turner, struggling against his rope ties and the pain of being strung across a saddle while traveling at a trot.

"Shut up, Turner. Want to stay tied up like that all day?" Nelson knew the area; it felt good to be traveling on Missouri soil again. When he crossed into Missouri, he had looked for Hagan but there was no sign of him. "Stopping just ahead. Then I'll set you up on that saddle."

"Don't have any money. Where you taking me? Who the hell are you?"

Nelson didn't answer the question. He pulled up in a thick stand of trees and stopped to untie the ropes holding Turner in the saddle. Turner's legs folded under him and he slumped to the ground.

"Stay down there," Nelson said, pulling the cover from Turner's head and pushing him flat on the ground with his boot.

"Shit . . . tying a man on a horse like that. Ain't human," he whined, pulling himself up by a stirrup to stand. "Pissed all over myself a hour ago."

"Might be doing a lot more of pissing if I shoot you," Nelson said, taking his own aim on a tree. "Going to need those legs working, so walk around, before I tie you up straight in that saddle for the rest of the ride."

"Damn it. Who are you?" Turner demanded again.

"Captain Nelson Paintier to you, Lieutenant Turner." Pointing his .44 at the man. "Get your hands out in front. I'm tying you back up. Going to ride along-side me. Make a break for it and I'll kill you."

"Ain't never going to hold me in no Rolla Stockade."

He's going to wish like hell he was back in Rolla, when he gets to the hawksbill camp, thought Nelson. He urged the mustang into a trot. "Keep up, Turner. Army shoots deserters and escapees."

Nelson had taken care to fill both his saddlebags with food before leaving Lawrence. He would stop midday to feed them both and rest the horses.

Nelson wasn't surprised that all the houses and barns along the trace were gone. Nothing standing but rock walls and blackened fireplaces, monuments to the Federal Army's Order 11 in 1863. General Ewing cleaned out the guerrilla supporters in three western Missouri counties by burning out all the people, regardless of who they supported. Few people had returned, unwilling to sign the loyalty pledge.

The trip to Lawrence had taken more than several days. Dealing with Turner on the way back would take longer.

"Riding late tonight." He urged Turner to keep up.

Nelson had been leading Turner's horse in the dark for two hours when he heard the sound of water rippling across the trace. Riding downstream for a short distance he stopped the horses and got Turner out of the saddle before tying him to a tree.

"You got room to sit or stand, Turner. Doesn't matter," Nelson said, dropping the saddles from the horses and leading them to water. He didn't want to risk a campfire attracting attention so out came the hardtack and jerked-meat.

"You chased me clear to Kansas. Thought I'd killed you back in the brush," Turner said.

"Shot a friend of mine back there," Nelson said as he checked Turner's ropes before thinking about sleep. "Give me any trouble; I'm going to tie you to the back legs of my mustang. See how quiet you can be then."

"Fuck, you . . . ain't regular army. Why you doing this to me?"

"Something you did up Jeff City way. Got right under my craw. You took the pledge to be an officer, not a murderer."

"Took that pledge before they killed my Pa, taught me an eye for an eye," Turner said.

Nelson looked at him in disgust, thinking he'll change his mind about that when I get him to the hawksbill. "Pa teach you to skin a man too?"

"He was one of Bloody Bill Anderson's bushwhackers. Don't matter how he died. They were raiding and killing all along the Missouri River."

"That boy was Jim Hagan's son. Ever hear of Jim Hagan? Believe he's looking for you all over southern Missouri."

Turner got quiet.

CHAPTER 24

"Come on Turner, get on that horse. We've got a long ride ahead today."

"Paintier, you better get me the hell back to that stinking Rolla stockade. Hagan catches us out here he'll hang us both."

"Oh! Now you want to go back there? Plenty of time for hanging when I get you back."

"They'll never hang me. Find out confederates killed my Pa, they'll acquit me," Turner said.

"Your Pa. Is he the Turner who ran the grocery at Loose Creek?"

"Did you know him?" asked the surprised Turner.

"Yep. Stopped in there and met him about two weeks after you killed that boy. You lying sack of shit." Pulling up the horses at the sight of what was ahead.

A troop of mounted federal cavalry stood blocking the trace. Nelson was afraid he was in trouble for the incident at Rolla, there was no way he could outrun the cavalry, and still drag Turner along. Instead, he rode right to their front and stopped to salute the officer in command.

"Captain Nelson Paintier, sir. Returning my prisoner to Jefferson Barracks for court-martial."

"Raise your hands, Captain Paintier. Both of you are now our prisoners," the federal officer said. He ordered his men to strip Nelson of his weapons.

"Hold on, what the hell, I have written orders in my saddle bags to return this man to Jefferson Barracks," Nelson said.

"That the same order you tried to hoodwink my Rolla troops with, Captain Paintier?" the officer asked. "A two day ride back to Rolla will, give you time to think about a visit to the stockade there."

With troops on both sides and chains on their wrists Nelson and Turner began the trip back to Rolla. Wasn't much doubt in Nelson's mind, he had gone too far in helping Hagan get his revenge.

Turner soon started in on Nelson, "Goin' to like sharing a cell with you. I'll catch you asleep some night. Make up for the fucking ride tied across this damn horse."

"Shut up Turner," Nelson said, "We aren't back there yet."

"At least it ain't you takin' me," Turner said.

Nelson had planned to wait for dark to try to escape, taking Turner with him. The troops wouldn't have a place to hold him when they stopped for the day. Nelson thought he still had a chance to get away until the troops chained him to Turner.

Nelson knew the odds had gotten better when the officer broke off the first sergeant and four men to escort their prisoners back. The officer commented to the first sergeant that he and the rest of the troops would continue west toward Bates County to put down some unrest.

An hour of daylight remained when the first sergeant ordered the troops off the trace into a clearing that appeared to have been used as their camp before.

Nelson felt relief when they unlocked his chains to get him down from his horse. His relief didn't last long; they chained his arms around a tree with Turner on the other side. He watched as the sergeant posted two of his men as sentries, out twenty yards from the camp. He ordered two-hour rotations for the guards. The other two started a small fire to make coffee. No one offered coffee or food.

Tied to a tree again for the night rubbed Nelson the wrong way, he couldn't sleep hugging a damn tree. He finally found a way to get his arms low enough on the tree to lie down. He didn't get to sleep because Turner kept chuckling and jerking on the chains to torment him.

"Sergeant, take these chains off long enough for Turner to take a piss," Nelson said.

"Oh, Captain sir. I'm sure he can piss just where he is. Word is, they're going to hang him back in Saint Louis. He'll for sure know what warm piss feels like running down his leg then," said the sergeant, chuckling at his own humor.

It got quiet after that. Sometime after midnight Nelson heard the sound of two head splitting blows at the perimeter of the camp. He watched a shadow cross the campfire and stop with a pistol to the head of the first sergeant. Hagan had returned.

"Get up, tell your two men to keep their heads under their blanket if they don't want to die tonight," Hagan said, shoving the sergeant toward Turner and Nelson. "Unchain both of them." Hagan's men were quick to bring up Nelson and Turner's mounts. Nelson recovered his .44 and carbine and saddled the mustang. Hagan had put the chains back on Turners arms.

"Who the hell is this?" Turner demanded, not realizing the short path to hell he was traveling on.

With the five soldiers hogtied and left at the camp, Hagan and his men led the way south. They had Turner's horse wedged in between two of the riders.

"Head for Buffalo River and the hawksbill," Hagan told the riders. "Men all gathered back there when we didn't show up. Your woman's there waiting for you too, Nelson."

CHAPTER 25

Nelson could see Anne watching their approach and breaking into a run when she realized he was there. He jumped from the saddle before his horse stopped to take her into his arms.

"I wasn't sure you would get back," she said, holding him tightly in her embrace.

"When they left with you I thought I would have to search all of southern Missouri to have you back in my arms," whispered Nelson, lifting her hair to caress her neck.

"Oh, Nelson, what are they going to do to that man?" Anne asked.

"They'll kill him for what he did to Hagan's son."

"Will it be a quick death?"

"Hagan will make him suffer just like his son did. Don't think Hagan will listen to me about taking Turner back to hang. I'll try talking to him," Nelson said. He crossed the camp to find Hagan.

"Hagan, can we talk about this?" Nelson said.

"Stay out of this, Nelson. He's mine now." He led the chained Turner toward a log circle in the center of the camp. "Sit, damn it."

Hagan's men sat waiting for the set-in-stone trial to start. Nelson and Anne stood behind the men not sure what was going to happen next.

"Red, you able to stand long enough to try this piece of shit?" Hagan asked, watching as Red pushed himself up from the log seat.

Red pointed at Turner and asked, "You got anything to say, dead man, before we start this trial?"

"Won't make no difference . . . all you are just like the ones we killed," Turner said, standing in defiance and shaking his fist and spitting toward Red.

"Difference is we got you," Red said. "You'd be dead now if we wasn't fair."

"Hagan says we got a witness to what you did, Turner," Red said pointing toward Nelson. "Tell him what you know, Nelson."

"Hagan said for me to stay out of this," Nelson said.

"Still a Billy Yankee, ain't you, Captain?" Hagan said. "You brought him out of Lawrence. You should have something to say at his trial."

"The Western command had him put in the stockade for murdering your son," Nelson said. "No man should die the way your son did, not even the one you have on trial." Nelson felt Anne tighten her grip on his side.

"That's good enough for me to get a vote," Red said. Each of Hagan's men showed Turner a thumb down.

"You got anything to say, Turner?" Hagan asked.

"Won't make no difference what I say," Turner said.

"Might make a difference how quick you die," Hagan said.

"Glad I skinned the little bushwhacking fuck. I'd do it all over," Turner said.

"Take off his chains," Hagan said. "Give him an empty pistol and one shell to put in his pocket."

Turner stood staring at Hagan, holding the empty pistol between both of his hands.

"You got one hour, before we come after you," Hagan said. "Best use that cartridge on yourself. If you don't I'm going to drag you back here and hang you over the cliff upside down with your guts hanging out."

"Run- it's your only chance, Turner," Red said.

Turner shook his fist at Nelson, "You're nothing but a fucking bushwhacker now." Turner disappeared running down the ridge toward the valley.

"Nobody goes after him till I say so," Hagan said. "Get the pole ready to hang him out over the hawksbill."

Nelson tried again to talk to Hagan and convince him that Turner should hang at Jefferson Barracks; it would set an example for the rest of the army. Hagan listened, but wanted more than an eye for an eye from Turner. When the hour had passed Hagan turned to Nelson.

"Bring him back, Nelson. If I go I'll kill him out there. I want him to die here on the hawksbill."

"He's not going to use that bullet on himself, he's a coward," Nelson said, "Doesn't believe what you threaten him with."

"You bring him back and he'll find out, won't he?"

The broken branches along the path led Nelson down the valley toward Buffalo River. Turner was running like a crazy man, with no thought of the trail he left to follow. Twice Nelson found spots of blood where Turner had taken a hard fall on the path. Two hours passed before Nelson reached the river. He knew Turner wouldn't try to cross the raging white water of the Buffalo.

"It's you that came after me?" Turner's voice came from behind Nelson. Turning he came face to face with Turner no more than thirty feet away, pistol cocked and aimed.

"Hagan told you . . . best use that shot on yourself," Nelson said. "He's not going to show you any mercy."

"Ain't goin' back. Gonna kill the sonofabitch that got me in this mess."

"Then take your shot. The way your hand is shaking . . . I'm waiting," Nelson said, seeing the smoke from the shot even before hearing the sound. The shock of the bullet passing his side moved the edge of his shirt.

"My turn now." Nelson pointed his .44 at Turners chest. *'I'd shoot him now if Anne's safety wasn't at stake.'*

"Head back up the trail, Turner. Not goin' to drag you, instead I'm going to shoot you in the arms if you don't do what I say."

"He's gonna . . . skin me."

"Walk, Turner."

Turner stumbled into the guerrilla camp with Nelson pressing him forward. Several hands grabbed for Turner forcing his back to a tree.

"Drag him to the hawksbill." Hagan said. "Turkey buzzards already circling waiting for your stinkin' guts, Turner."

"Don't follow, Anne," Nelson said, showing her his open hand.

"Just shoot him out there on the hawksbill, Captain," whispered Anne.

"Hagan would never let us leave here alive if I do," Nelson said, surprised at Anne's bluntness.

Hagan's men dragged the sobbing Turner through the woods to the waiting precipice. A long pine tree pole braced against two boulders stood ready to swing the upside-down Turner out over the edge of the Buffalo River canyon. Nelson stared at the fall from the hawksbill and wished Hagan would just throw Turner over the edge instead of gutting him first. Gutting him turned Nelson's stomach, bringing back memories of battle field wounds, men left to try and push their guts back inside in hope life would stay, perhaps only for tomorrow's sunrise. Still they prayed and cried out

"Ma . . . Ma . . . I'm coming . . . coming home." Nelson realized he could not stop Hagan from getting his revenge and justice.

Hagan's men stripped Turner and held him flat on the ground before tying his feet to the end of the long pole.

Hagan approached Nelson first.

"I'm telling you again, stay out of this. Understand?" Hagan said. "I'll kill you on the spot."

Nelson watched Turner shake and twist from side to side trying to get the ties on his feet loose. Hagan walked to Turner's side and took a skinning knife from the sheath at his side.

"Lift the pole. Get him off the ground," Hagan said.

The pivot of the pole raised Turner into the air, only the tips of his fingers touched the ground.

"Look at me, Turner. Goin' open your belly wide. Your guts'll fall right over your face," Hagan said. "Then leave you hanging out there over the hawksbill alive. Them circling buzzards know what's comin'. Start with your eye balls and pick you clean to the bone."

Hagan reached across Turner's belly, the edge of the skinning knife pressed against bare flesh. Nelson lifted his pistol. The snap of the rifle shot came at the same time Hagan's knife parted the skin. The back of Turner's head went flying out over the canyon. Hagan dropped the knife on the ground and spun toward Nelson.

"You bitch," Hagan shouted, racing past Nelson and slapping the rifle from Anne's hands, before he knocked her to the ground.

"There! The terror you caused him paid for your son," Anne said.

Hagan pointed his pistol at Nelson, "Take her. Get out of here. Before I kill you both."

CHAPTER 26

The moonlit night found Nelson and Anne more than fifteen miles from the hawksbill camp. They had ridden the horses at a run wanting to get far away from Hagan and his men. Their horses were too tired to climb the trail over the mountain to leave the Buffalo Valley, so they had pulled up on a river sandbar for the night. Neither had spoken for the last hour.

"I saw you go for the pistol," Anne said. "He would have killed you."

"I almost died anyway from the shock of seeing you standing there with a smoking rifle," Nelson said, shaking his head from side to side.

"Will they come after us?"

"No, I think Hagan is glad it's over with Turner."

"What about the pardons, Nelson?" Anne asked while unsaddling her horse.

"I think he understands the pardons represent his only way to ever go back home and start over. We'll have to wait and see if he comes for them," Nelson said taking the two horses to drink and returning to hobble them to graze the higher riverbank.

"I haven't been near a bath for way too long," Anne said dropping her clothes as she ran to the fast running stream.

The image of Anne's tall body and long midnight black hair bathed in the moonlight erased all the bad things that had tortured Nelson for the last week. He dropped to the sand, sitting quietly with his arms wrapped around his knees, watching, trying to see way more of Anne than the flowing river would allow. He loved watching her duck her head and come up to throw the long strands of hair over her shoulder.

"Are you going to sit up there alone forever, Captain?"

She would not have to ask the question twice. Nelson's boots were already off sitting beside him, the rest of his clothes were strung between the boots and the river's edge. The cold water stung him, but only for a second. When he got near, he wrapped her in his arms. Too much had happened that day, both only wanted the embrace; an embrace that would warm them for days to come. They held each other tightly for more than a few minutes.

"You know I'm going to be a scandal in Steelville, don't you? They will kick me out of the school for being with you; but I'm still glad you came along into my life, Captain Nelson Paintier."

"I'm glad too, Miss Ruth Anne Gordon. Now kiss me again, scandalous woman." They spent the night hungry, for more of each other.

The war, Union Soldiers, guerrilla troops, had all stripped the farms of cattle and crops, making things hard for families who had to hide what little food they had to survive. Nelson had buried most of the gold he brought from Jefferson Barracks, but he still carried enough to bring out some of the hidden food on the way north. It would be dangerous approaching farms for help, even families with the same name were divided in their support of the north or the south. Ambushes were frequent, bitter killings of cousins had happened throughout the Buffalo River Valley.

With morning's light, Nelson again went swimming in the river. In a few minutes he had four large fresh water mussels lying on the bank. If they were going to have anything to eat it would have to come from those shells for now. Nelson watched Anne shaking her head from side to side, no, no.

"Coons eat them, you know," Nelson said slipping back into his pants and going to work with his hunting knife to open the hard shell mussels.

"Enjoy your morning meal," Anne said starting to think that the clean mussel meat could be all they would get for the rest of the day. Nelson lifted the mussel from the half shell on his knife and offered the dripping bite to Anne.

"Go ahead, you first, Captain."

He didn't wait, but took the whole mussel down in one swallow.

"Not bad, Anne. Pickins' may be slim the rest of the day."

"All right, don't laugh if this slime gets stuck in my throat," Anne said.

They were both hungry, so twice more Nelson went back into the river for mussels. After they forced them down, and saddled the horses, they headed over the mountain to leave the Buffalo River behind them. Nelson rode hoping to find a farm with a big garden. They were not that lucky. The day ended with both of them still hungry.

No need to delay, they were saddled and riding at dawn. Nelson preferred the lesser traveled trails that led north, hoping to find farms that had been spared the wrath of the war.

It was midday when they topped a ridge and saw the weather-beaten house with broken panes in both front windows. A heavy moss layer had started to fill in the uneven spaces in the wooden roof. The open front door made the house look like it had been deserted for years. Only part of the corral fence on the north side of the house was there. Empty fence posts stood alone, the rails that keep livestock inside were gone.

"Looks like they used part of the corral for firewood last winter," Nelson said riding to the edge of the fence.

"Nelson, there's a woman on her knees, working a little garden," Anne said.

Nelson took up the slack in his reins, "Get ready to ride, Anne. I just heard a hammer being pulled back inside the house," whispered Nelson.

A child's voice from the house, "Ain't no garden she's doin'. Trying to bury a dead baby. Best get on out of here. Ain't nothin' here no more."

"Talk to him, Anne. Woman's voice will be better."

"I'll help your mother. Help her bury her child," Anne said. "We didn't come to steal. Just hungry like you must be."

A shirtless skin and bones body of a boy carrying a rusty muzzle loader came around the house. Rings of dirt circled his chest, his bare feet were the color of the red clay yard. The boy stood the musket against the clap board side of the house, and walked up to Anne and her horse, stopping with his hand on her boot. His tears made puddles in the dirt that covered both his cheeks. "Ma just been sittin' lookin' at that dead baby all night," the boy said. "She killed him 'fore he starved to death."

Anne and Nelson both swung down from their mounts, to the boy's side.

"She killed her baby!" Anne said.

"All us starvin'. I've been hidin' thinkin' she's goin' to kill me too."

"Your mother needs you, son. Help with hunting for food," said Nelson.

"Had the gun hid, when they come. Took the little bit of powder and lead that was left with them. Can't shoot nothin' to eat no more."

"Who came? What else did they take?" Nelson asked.

"Ma called them neighbors, before they came. Called us Secesh traitors. They beat grandpa to death with his walkin' stick."

Nelson didn't know what to say, only slowly shook his head.

"I'm proud of my Grandpa, mister. He cussed that man, before he went. Told him hell would be too good for him and his kin."

"I'm going to help now. Help your Ma bury the little one," Nelson said.

Anne went to the mother and took her to sit on a rock ledge behind the house. Nelson walked with his arm around the boy to join them.

"Buried her dad over by the edge of the field. She wants to bury the baby so it will be near him," Anne said, sitting next to the grieving woman.

Nelson found a broken shovel in the yard and headed toward the pile of stones and the narrow plank-cross carved to mark the boy's grandfather's last resting place. Without asking, he dug the shallow grave for the child beside the pile of stones. When he finished he walked back to Anne and the mother.

"When she's ready," Nelson said softly to Anne.

Without a word, the mother stood, walked to the body of the baby and lifted it from the quilt.

"Ain't got no other way to keep the boy warm when winter comes to this mountain, goin' to need this quilt," the woman said, carrying the naked baby toward the freshly dug grave.

At the edge of the grave she passed the rigid body to Nelson's arms. The decay that had begun in the day's heat gripped his stomach. The smell of death he could not forget, it flowed over every battlefield he had fought on and lasted for days. He knelt at the side of the shallow hole and slowly lowered the baby to the bottom. He stood and backed away to the side of the boy.

"Go ahead, cover him up," the mother said. "No need to pray. All that prayin' we done since the start of the war brought us nothin' but death and nothin' to feed my brats. It brought a church prayin' neighbor to kill my pa and steal all we had to eat. Ain't prayin' no more."

With tears in her eyes Anne gripped Nelson's arm whispering, "Wait." She turned and ran to her saddlebags, taking out a clean white blouse she had been saving. Returning to the side of the grave she handed the blouse to Nelson.

"Please," Anne said.

Nelson again lifted the lifeless body and placed it inside the blouse. Nelson and Anne scooped a small handful of red clay and slowly sprinkled it over the baby's body. The little brother followed their lead. The mother turned away, and ran into the house.

"My momma is sad. She just don't know how to show it anymore, mister," the boy said.

CHAPTER 27

After Nelson and Anne finished the burial, they walked back to the house arm in arm.

"Do you think she killed her own baby?" Anne asked.

"She probably hasn't eaten for days. They must have taken her cow, and her own milk dried up, there wouldn't be anything she could do to feed a baby."

"We have to help them. Can we take them with us?"

"We could if she would go. I'm thinking of paying a visit to her thieving neighbor. Maybe getting some food back for them."

"Don't ride into more than you can handle, Nelson."

Knowing he would have to somehow put food on the table today, Nelson unsaddled the horses and hobbled them to graze the sparse grass, then drew his rifle from the scabbard. Digging to the bottom of his saddlebags, he came up with a ball of heavy string that he handed to the boy.

"Let's go, son. See what's left of the wildlife here on the mountain," Nelson said, heading off toward the woods. Within a half mile he motioned for the boy to come sit by a tree. "Looks like a spot squirrels will be coming to feed," He sat down beside the boy and showed him the acorns split by the squirrels.

In a few minutes, Nelson pointed to a large oak tree just in front of them and whispered, "Hear the noise? It's a squirrel climbing on the bark; he's up there on the other side of the tree hiding from us. You slip around to the other side, make a little noise and he'll come around for me to shoot."

The red squirrel was quick to move around the tree away from the noise the boy was making. Nelson leveled the rifle and with a shot to the squirrel's small head harvested the start of dinner.

"Wow damn, wish I could shoot like that," the boy said.

The boy was smiling and carrying the rifle for Nelson when they headed back to the house with four cleanly shot squirrels. "Thanks for letting me shoot, mister, Sorry I missed him though," the boy said.

"Lots harder to hit a squirrel with a rifle than a shotgun. Takes even more practice to shoot them in the head," Nelson said.

On the way back Nelson showed the boy places where rabbits had made paths going through the brush and grass. Using the cord they had brought, he taught the boy how to set snares that would not fail to get him rabbits.

"Be sure you check the snares twice a day, otherwise a fox or wolf will steal your catch," Nelson told the boy.

"I will, maybe even more often when we get really hungry," the boy said.

"Can you clean squirrels?" Nelson asked knowing that he needed to hunt for bigger game for the family to live on.

"Sure, cleaned them all the time, 'fore runnin' out of any way to shoot 'em."

"Ok, I'm going to reload and head down the ridge toward the water. May get lucky and spot a deer when they move near sunset. Tell the ladies to go ahead and cook the squirrels, don't wait for me."

Nelson knew both armies had done their parts in cleaning out most of the big game in the Buffalo River area. He hoped to kill a deer to provide lasting food for the woman and boy. He reached the river and followed it upstream for a quarter mile before finding what he had been looking for, a worn trail of deer tracks to the riverbank. He backed off from the trail about twenty yards and crawled into a thick bunch of willows for cover. Night found him still watching the river's edge for prey. He settled back against the willows to wait for the morning.

Well before dawn Nelson sat alert and watched the trail. His luck got better at midmorning when a doe came down the trail and lowered her head to get a drink. Nelson's shot dropped the deer at the water's edge. After bleeding and gutting the kill, he headed up the mountain to get his horse for the carry. Anne and the boy met him halfway leading the horse.

"I heard the shot–thought it must be you," Anne said, handing him a skewered squirrel. "We roasted the squirrels last night. I saved this one for you."

"Hungry enough to eat raw deer, luck was with me, bagged a doe too big to carry out," Nelson said, giving Anne a hug and greeting the boy. "Might need all of us to get the deer up on the horse, it's heavy." Nelson chewed the squirrel meat off the bones as they went down the hill to the river.

With the doe finally over the horse's back, they climbed the steep hill back to the cabin. In back of the cabin, Nelson hung the deer from a tree to finish butchering it. He cut several steaks and carried them to Anne to cook for dinner. After he filled a tub of meat to be ground for sausage, he cut the rest into thin strips and took them to the woman to dry for jerky.

He said to the woman, "I need to know where to find the man that killed your father and stole your food."

"No! No, more killing goin' happen over me," she said.

"Then go with Anne and me. We can take you to any other family you have."

"This is our home. He's comin' back to us, soon."

"Your husband? How long's he been gone?"

"Two years now. They took him away to fight."

Nelson didn't ask about the baby. He knew the scars she must be wearing that came with the baby's conception, but still she didn't want to leave her mountain home.

The next morning Nelson and Anne waved goodbye to the woman and boy. He felt the large deer kill and the renewed spirit of the boy to provide rabbits would at least keep them alive for a while. They rode toward the Missouri Ozarks and Anne's burnt out home.

Joshua shouted his hello when they started down the steep hill into town. "Nelson, I was afraid you wouldn't come back," he dropped his rake and ran to meet them. "Where's my pa? Is he all right?"

"He's okay, Joshua. Don't know when he'll be coming back though," Anne said, leaving her saddle to hug the boy.

"Joshua, see you have some help cleaning up the burnt out house," Nelson said. He walked to Thomas and gripped his leather-hard hand. "Glad you decided to stay and give us a hand, Thomas."

"Thought you might help me learn to read if I stayed to help," Thomas said.

"We both will, Thomas." Anne said, "Guess we will have to fix up the barn to live in till I can get a house built."

"Mind if I lend a hand, young lady?" Nelson asked.

"Counting on it, mister," Anne said.

The next three weeks went fast, Nelson made several trips to the Iron Work's sawmill for lumber and building supplies. On his last trip he was able to hire two of the Iron Work's carpenters to help build the house. Nelson kept busy and didn't have time to think about Sheriff Spaid's men that had been out to kill him. During the first week of building, Mr. Oliver came looking for him and asked to talk to him alone.

"Nelson, Mrs. Oliver and I noticed a couple of strangers riding through town along Yadkin Creek while you were gone with Ms. Anne. They always rode up the hill checking on the school and the burnt out house. Then they rode on out of town after that. Think they were looking for you?"

"Might be. Some don't like the fact that I'm back in Steelville."

"We're glad you're here," Mr. Oliver said. "Going to take all the help we can get to rebuild from this flood and war, Nelson. Glad the boy could stay with us while you and Miss Anne were away. He kept wanting to run off after his dad again. We kept him busy helping to build our house."

"Thanks, Mr. Oliver. How's your house coming along?"

"Neighbors lent a hand. Moved what was left of it up the ridge away from the creek. I'll be safe up there next time it floods."

Nelson thanked him again for keeping Joshua, Anne joined them to give Mr. Oliver a fresh loaf of bread she had baked on the stove Thomas had set up in the lot back of the barn.

"Don't know what we would have done if you hadn't taken care of Joshua while we were gone," Anne said.

"Glad to do it for our school teacher. I'm a little embarrassed to ask, Miss Ruth, but is the nigger working here a slave?" Mr. Oliver asked.

"Was a slave, but he's a freedman now," Anne said, "Earning what we can pay him for helping us."

"That's good. I respect that. Some folk around here been talking, those folk have hoods hanging in their closets need your watching."

"Glad you let me know. I'm sure Thomas is aware of the hatred that exists and will do his best to avoid any trouble," Anne said. "Come back and bring Mrs. Oliver. We will put together what we can for a housewarming when the house is finished, and you are both invited."

Nelson and the builders had the house ready for the roof to be put on when Dyer rode into Steelville. Before Anne could even greet him, he pointed his finger at her. "Almost got us killed, up there at the hawksbill. Lucky Hagan let you ride out of there."

Anne didn't answer. She knew Dyer would calm down after a bit. She yelled for Joshua that his pa was there. The boy came around the house and ran to his father, grabbing him around the waist in a big hug.

The house sat ready for the roof, with all the material at hand and plenty of help. After talking it over with Anne, Nelson felt he could leave for a bit. He wasted no time before heading for Jefferson City. He needed a telegraph to send a notice to ship the printing press his deceased Saint Louis parents had willed to him.

He worried about the army looking for him but felt sure the Saint Louis army command had taken the heat off for the incidences with Lt. Turner. He had been given an open hand of cards to play. Whatever it took, the commander general had told him. He needed to notify the commander about the fact Turner was dead, and the pardons still needed to be awarded.

Nelson always liked riding into Jefferson City. From several miles away the granite capitol always stood out shining, there on the river bluff overlooking the Missouri River. He enjoyed watching the ferryboats make trips back and forth across the river. He didn't take time this trip to stop and enjoy the view. He rode on into town, early in the morning. He had to face his enemies and see what crawled out of the dirt.

Morning of April 15, 1865

After leaving his horse at a livery stable, he headed straight to the telegraph office; the operator arrived just as Nelson did, and unlocked the building right at eight o'clock. The code key on the desk was clicking before the operator had a chance to sit down and lift his pencil to start writing. When the operator finished writing the incoming message, he sat staring at the piece of paper in his hand. Nelson tapped the counter trying to attract his attention. The operator stood and turned toward Nelson. His arms and hands shook as he announced to the only person there, the President had been shot—assassinated. Nelson moved aside, in shock, as the operator bolted out the door, shouting to all, "Lincoln is dead!"

CHAPTER 28

Nelson watched the still clicking telegraph key, continuing its message to the empty operator's chair.

"Lincoln dead!" My God, he thought. So many had died fighting for Lincoln's vision, United States of America free of slavery in both the north and south. Now he's dead! Now Lincoln's dead. Lincoln had never offered a compromise to the south. Surely, the vice president would not offer one now, he reasoned.

Going north as a boy, fleeing for his life from the men in Steelville who wanted him dead had put him in a different world. New people had taken him in, still a boy needing guidance and wanting to learn other ways than those he had learned from his father and the men and women around southern Missouri.

Always in the south they had preached the nigger slaves were no more than savages to be treated as such. New ways, working with men both white and black, had taught him that both could exist and live free. And then the war, fighting beside the black men and leading them into battle, confirmed his belief in equality. They had repeatedly proven the courage and determination the south had always denied them. Lincoln dead! How could that be?

Before noon, the town's streets were flooded with wagons and buggies, people all trying to get the news and find out what had happened in Washington. Nelson knew Missouri had its share of Lincoln haters, people who wanted the war to go on and end with the state part of a new country controlled by the Confederacy. He needed to find out who in the capital city of Missouri wanted him dead.

Certain he blended well with the crowds, he went to the capitol first. Climbing the five marble steps, he stopped to read the engraved letters high on the wall of the building. "Built in 1838." The five thirty-inch solid marble columns majestically supported the upper balcony over the entrance. He entered the door that had been left open by the frantic crowd that milled in the streets.

The nearly empty building offered Nelson an opportunity to observe the names and offices of the men in the Missouri Government. He climbed the steps to the second floor corridor and strolled past the office doors left open by the rush out. He read the names and titles of the men in power. He thought of the many debates and arguments that must have raged between them on how to shape Missouri's position in the war, and always how to keep the fight away from their own homes and families.

He stopped in an open space between the offices to look out the windows at the Missouri River below. The ferryboat J.W. Spencer had reached the middle of the river. Black smoke poured from the two smoke stacks, a sure sign the captain had a full load on board and was in a big hurry to reach the capital city. Nelson could see more than a dozen wagons on the north side of the river still waiting for the boat to return. The news of Lincoln's death had gripped the countryside.

Two more offices remained at the end of the hall. The last office belonged to a senator, whose name was painted on the door. It was a name he remembered; someone from his past in Steelville. He felt his heartbeat speed up a notch. This judge had thrown him out of his chambers when he had gotten the courage to tell him that Mary, the slave girl, did not drown the Mockbee's baby. The judge's shouts still rang in Nelson's ears, "Get out! Get out, you nigger-loving little bastard!"

Nelson realized he would have to find out more about the senator before he could be sure he had sent the men who killed his father. He felt certain of one thing: this senator would not want Missouri to be any part of Lincoln's Union of States.

Back on the street he noticed the citizens had gathered in small groups, some talking softly, sadly, about the news of the day. Another group, mostly men, passed a flask from man to man. When he watched carefully he could see the men tip the flask in a half-hidden salute, the disrespect for the president showed on their faces and in the smiles and back-patting of their fellow pro-Confederates. Several squads of federal troops marched by Nelson and took up guard positions along the Capitol's front and the sidewalk leading there. Probably expecting trouble, thought Nelson.

The doors to the Methodist Church stood wide open as he passed going south down the street that led to the Union Hotel. Nelson turned back to the church and went in. The pews were nearly full; the minister stood in the pulpit speaking of the great loss to the country and then "A moment of silent prayer for our slain president."

Nelson slid into the closest pew and bowed his head with the congregation. His thoughts of the tall slender man he had once seen standing near General Grant for a picture saddeded Nelson as he thought of the terrible struggle the man had endured since becoming president. Nelson prayed silently: "God, let him rest in peace." When the minister asked the congregation to stand and sing, he got up and left the church.

The streets were crowded, but Nelson noticed a man half a block behind him start walking south at the same time he left the church. The clerk at the desk of the Union Hotel asked no questions when Nelson signed in using a fictitious name, and handed him a key to a room on the second floor.

No one had followed Nelson into the hotel, so he climbed the steps, went into his room locking the door behind, and collapsed on the bed. No way would he sit another minute, he finally had a bed. The first in some time for the weary soldier.

It was past midnight when the soft knock at the door awoke him. Rolling off the bed he gripped the smaller pistol he had brought for his trip to the city and crouched at the side of the door. A second knock and a voice said, "Captain Paintier? Open the door, sir."

He expected a lot of things to come with the knock, but the words "Captain Paintier" and "sir" were not part of them. Nelson realized opening the door could get him shot if he was wrong about who stood outside.

Carefully, without standing, he turned the key to unlock the door, and then slid along the floor to the side of a heavy dresser. If somebody wanted to kill him, they would have a fight on their hands in his dark room.

"I'm coming in, Captain Paintier, carrying a lantern in one hand, the other is empty, sir."

Nelson cocked his pistol and pointed directly at the heart of the man who came through the door into his room.

"Hold the lantern higher with both hands. I want to see your face," Nelson said, moving from behind the dresser. "Shut the door behind you, lock it."

"Commander knew you would show up in Jefferson City sooner or later. Thought you might be in over your head with things going on down south with Turner and all," the man said.

"Who are you?" Nelson asked, his pistol aimed at the stranger.

"Name's Edwin, don't use last names in the service branch I'm in."

"Ok, Edwin. Put the lantern on the table and sit; I'll stand back a ways. Does command know Turner's dead?"

"They thought that would be the case. Since you handed him over to Hagan and his men."

"Hagan didn't take the pardon, but most of his men are tired of the bushwhacker life, always on the run either chasing or being chased."

"Troops have been ordered to stand down on looking for you. Commander said he gave you orders to bring in Hagan one way or another and he still means it."

"Will Lincoln's death change anything with my orders?" Nelson dropped into the chair beside the stranger.

"Nothing will change for a while; it will take the new president some time to get around to changing field officers," Edwin said.

"In your report, tell them someone in the state government is out to kill me. Sent men after me twice. It's nothing to do with Hagan and the pardons, it's about the book I'm writing and the wrongs that happened in Steelville before the war."

"Know who that someone might be?"

"Do now. Judge from Crawford County; he's now a senator. Name's Saunders. He sent a crooked sheriff to burn us out when I was a boy and killed my dad in the fight."

"We know about Senator Saunders. Suspect he and some of his henchmen have been running guns south to the Confederates. Did you know he's got his name up to run for governor?"

Now Nelson knew, clear as could be. The senator was trying to escape the past and the things he had caused in Crawford County. Stop the book and shut down old history from being revisited, just that simple. Oh yes, kill Nelson Paintier along the way.

"Been assigned here since the war started. Plan to keep an eye on Saunders and what he's up to," said Edwin. "Best you put an end to Hagan and his raiding; it would go a long way to explain your busting into the fort at Rolla."

"Heading back in the morning, don't know if Hagan will be so easy to find this time. Tell Command I still understand the mission, and I know Hagan's heart isn't into the raiding anymore."

"Good luck, Captain."

With the federal spy gone, Nelson felt better armed to face the man and the men who had been sent after him. Hunt out Sheriff Spaid . . . Spaid . . . as he dropped into the feather mattress already asleep.

CHAPTER 29

With a cup of coffee, two eggs and a steak filling his belly, Nelson headed back for the telegraph office. Most of the local people that rushed to town at the word of Lincoln's death had gone home. Nearing the top of the steep hill that defined the downtown for Jefferson City, a squad of federal troops passed him marching at double time headed for the Missouri River just down from his hotel. A lot of rush to get down there, thought Nelson.

The telegraph operator sat at his code key clicking away trying to get caught up on the pile of messages he had waiting. One message on the top of the pile caught Nelson's attention. The message ran a full page of text, nothing in it made any sense, it was code, for sure. It was addressed to a name in Saint Louis he remembered at Jefferson Barracks. It was signed simply "E." The agent had relayed his information on to his commander.

"Quite a stack of messages you got," Nelson said.

"Yep," the operator said, picking up the stack in front of Nelson and slipping them under his elbow. "Bunch of them came in late last night. I spent the night here just trying to catch up."

"Going to leave one more for you," Nelson said, picking up a pencil and writing out the message to the Saint Louis shipping company that had been holding his printing press.

"Dear Sir, Please ship the Lombard Press you have been holding for me to Jefferson City by steam ship. Notify me by mail at Steelville, Mo when the shipment is to leave. Name of steamship and time of arrival in J.C. Sincerely Nelson Paintier."

"Any other news from Washington?" Nelson asked, handing his message to the telegraph operator with the required twenty-five cent fee.

"Must be crazy there. Looking for an actor, named Booth, that shot Lincoln. Everyone's out to hang him."

"Stick this message on that pile under your arm," Nelson said, "Would like for it to remain private."

"I'd lose my job if I didn't," the operator said, turning back to the clattering code key.

With his goals met in Jefferson City, Nelson headed for his horse and the trip to Steelville. Halfway to the livery stable he saw the federal troops coming back from the riverfront. They were carrying a stretcher with a body on it. He sidestepped off the boardwalk to get a glance at who they were carrying.

"Move off the street, mister," said a first sergeant leading the troops. "Man's about as dead as he can get."

Nelson saw the grey face of the body on the stretcher, a man he had just met last night. Edwin had been shot in the forehead and tossed in the river. Nelson realized someone must have made a connection with his coming to town; it had gotten the secret federal agent killed. They had been on to his being in town since he got there yesterday morning. He had been careless not noticing anyone else following when he went to the hotel the night before. Now he realized, Spaid and the senator's men would be waiting to ambush him when he went south. He hurried to the stable, checked that his weapons were working, saddled the big gelding, and headed for the river landing.

Only one chance, catch the ferry and go north into Callaway County. With any luck, without them close on his heels a turn to either the east or west would be possible. Ferryboats operated all up and down the Missouri River, so he could get back across the river later.

The ferry's pilot had just closed the gate when he reached Lohman's Landing. With the offer of a good tip the gates were opened back up for him. Nelson led the horse to the back of the boat and watched the gates close as two riders rushed up trying to get on board. It was too late for the men following Nelson to get on the ferry; it had pulled away from the landing for the north bank of the river. He had his head start.

CHAPTER 30

With the ferry docked on the north shore of the river, Nelson headed across the mile long stretch of Missouri River bottomland, headed for the bluff road. He thought first about going west to Boonville and crossing back across the river there, but realized that would add days of travel time to his trip home. He had to head east and look for an out of the way river crossing somewhere around the mouth of the Osage River or further east.

The roads along the north bluffs were well traveled so his tracks would be hard to follow there. Nelson felt sure the men would be watching for him at the ferry crossing just out from the German settlement of Hermann, so he had to find a way across the Missouri at another place, the river was way too wide and dangerous to try and swim the horse across; he would need a boat or raft to cross.

Ten miles from the Jefferson City ferry crossing he found the answer to getting across the river without being detected. Heavy logging of the timber along the river area had made it necessary to have a steam driven barge to push the logs across the river and up into the slower Osage River to a sawmill. He found the owner of the barge on the end of a bucksaw cutting a three-foot thick walnut log into sections for transporting.

"Hey there, mister. I hear from your neighbors that you might be planning a river crossing sometime today?" Nelson yelled.

"What's on your mind, young fellow?" the barge owner asked, stopping his sawing and wiping his forehead with the dirty towel draped over his shoulder.

"Need to be on the other side tonight and I'm willing to pay you for the trip," Nelson said, not wishing to say any more about his reasons for crossing the river.

"Log business slowed down, North was buying a lot of lumber from us over in the town of Osage to make boxcars, but slowed down a lot since the war's ended. So how much you figure you could pay if we was willing to bring the steam up on the barge for you?"

Nelson didn't quibble; he took a gold piece from behind his gun belt and flipped it to the man.

"Get down, take a rest, steam be up in about an hour. We keep coals hot on her all the time. Planned on making another trip over to Osage this afternoon to see a gal anyway."

"Quicker you get going the better," Nelson said, dismounting and leading the mustang to the riverbank. The river looked like one huge muddy field, turning and boiling along the bank with whirlpools rising every few hundred feet. Nelson never wanted to be caught in whirlpools again.

The little steam barge sat rope tied, front and back, to large river sycamore trees. A narrow board walkway was the only way to board it. Nelson had crossed many wooden bridges with the horse so he didn't expect any problems getting him on board the boat.

"We going to need to hoist that horse on board?" the owner asked, pointing to the log lift rigged on the bank.

"Hope not, horse will go wherever I go. The walkway's really narrow, looks strong, so we're just going to have to try," Nelson said.

"Go ahead; get him on board if he'll go."

Nelson looked again at the walkway and knew that he wouldn't like making the twenty-foot walk over it any more than his horse. "Reckon I could use one of those bridles that you have up on your mule team?" Nelson asked.

"Sure could, mister."

"Big eyeshades on each side, just let him look straight ahead," Nelson said.

With the workhorse bridle on the mustang, Nelson led him to the front edge of the walkway. Without pausing, he stepped on the walk and never looked back. The big roan nearly ran over him pushing him to hurry across onto the barge.

"Get the horse settled down, the steam makes a lot of noise when she gets run up in the current," the owner said.

"Just stay off that whistle and he should be okay." Nelson said.

With the steam pressure up, the owner's helper untied the ropes from the sycamores. The strong river current whipped the front of the barge from the bank and pointed it downstream. The barge's engine let out two bursts of steam before beginning to turn the paddlewheel at the stern. The slap-slap of the wheel digging into the muddy water slowly brought the front of the barge around and got it heading across the river. Nelson stood with his hand rubbing the mustang's neck to help keep him calm.

Twenty minutes passed before the barge entered the mouth of the Osage River. Upstream a little less than a mile the owner guided the barge up solid against a large dock. The town of Osage looked quiet, a couple teams of horses tied in front of what looked like the general store was all Nelson could see.

Walking the horse off the barge, Nelson thanked the owner before riding through the town and onto a trail heading south to the Ozarks. He watched behind as he rode, after half a day's ride no one was following; he had eluded the men following him in Jefferson City. The men would try and head him off somewhere before Steelville. He rode on.

Nelson knew anyone who waited for him would expect him to ride in from the west or north, so he rode miles out of the way to approach Steelville from the east. The way was clear. He rode up to the back of the barn and the nearly complete house they were building for Anne. She saw him first and dropped a handful of laundry on the ground as she ran to wrap her arms around him.

"We heard this morning about the president being assassinated," she said, with her head pressed to his chest, "I was so worried about you."

"I missed you, Anne. Shouldn't have left so suddenly."

"Finding out who is behind nearly burning us up, you needed to go," Anne said, taking his hand and leading him toward the new house. "Come see the stove I found for the kitchen. The family left and said I could have it, it was too heavy for them to take in their wagon."

After Anne had a chance to show him the stove and house they went to the front where Dyer and Thomas were working to add a small porch. Nelson was eager to explain what had happened in Jefferson City and tell them he knew they were all in danger.

"Got chased out of Jefferson City by two men who wanted to kill me. A lot more is going on in Jefferson City than just hatred for me. A senator and Sheriff Spaid are running illegal guns south selling them to the Confederacy. An agent from army command paid me a visit, let me know command was aware of my capturing Turner, and they said I had the go ahead to do whatever it took to bring in Hagan. Next morning the agent was found dead, floating in the river."

"Damn! By the way Red come in with a message from Hagan while you were gone," Dyer said. "Hagan wants to know terms of the pardon."

"That's the best news I've heard in a long while. Can you set up a meeting with him?" Nelson asked.

"Hagan's been moving back north after leaving Buffalo River. Expect we wouldn't have to travel very far to have a meeting," Dyer said. "I'll see if I can get word out to him."

"Settle down, Captain. You just rode in from one chase," Anne said. "Joshua wants to see you. Maybe not as much as I do, however."

Nelson pulled Anne into a hug, holding the side of his head to hers. He knew she was right. He needed to get his priorities in order. Safety for Anne and the boy came first in his mind.

CHAPTER 31

Carrying his fishing pole and a stringer loaded with five big bluegills, Joshua trudged up the long hill to Anne's new house. He broke into a run when he saw Nelson in front of the house. He dropped the stringer on the hillside.

"Joshua, you look wetter than a snappin' turtle that just crawled out of the water," Dyer said, pointing at the boy as he ran to give Nelson a hug.

"I was afraid you wasn't comin' back," Joshua said, backing away from the hug that had come from the boy still in him.

"I'll always come back, this town is my home again. Now head back and get those fish, Anne will need them for dinner tonight."

With dinner over, Joshua pumped water from the well to wash the dishes; Nelson and Anne walked down the hill, and through the flood damaged buildings that were part of the town center.

"I always did like to walk along this creek," Anne said. "I thought the flood would change my mind about that."

"Not many folks going to rebuild down here. Moving up on the north hillside it looks like," Nelson said, lifting Anne in his arms and carrying her across the creek.

"Did you know they buried the slave girl up there? A rocky place near the edge of the bluff. No one even marked her grave."

"I'd like to go up there some time soon. Be a place for me to think about what I want to write about her and what happened."

"Bunch of the town hoodlums were up there last year, burnt a cross near where she is buried. They claimed she's a ghost haunting the town."

"The ghost of the girl that I write about in my book will haunt the guilty ones for a long time."

"Come on, mister, there's a little ledge that sticks out just up the way. We can sit there," Anne said, dropping his hand and running ahead.

Nelson followed at a slow run, his leg had healed and the exercise felt good. She encouraged him to hurry and join her on the ledge. He slipped onto the ledge and pushed tightly against her side. His love for Anne had come on so fast; he wanted to know all about her and her life as a schoolteacher. They talked and talked on through the night, sharing feelings and their past, until they saw the first rays of the sun start to come over the east ridge. Morning found them back at the house. Nelson dropped onto the cot set up for him in the barn, Anne was on a new bed trying to sleep, in a room with nothing covering the window.

Collecting his notes and writing material, Nelson left in the afternoon for the hill across the creek. He explained to Anne where he was going to write. He climbed the steep north side of the valley and walked along the rim of the hill looking for Mary's grave. When he found part of the burnt cross he knew her grave would be close. Most of the rocks that had been covering the grave lay scattered in front of the cross. Nelson spent the next hour placing them back on the desecrated grave of the slave girl.

He wasn't a man who stopped to pray a lot, but still, he stood silently remembering the hanging happening right before him down there in the valley. He knelt alongside the rock pile, and then sat on the rocky hillside beside Mary's resting place. He wanted to continue his book:

Her screams caused me to jump to my feet and rush around the brambles. She stumbled into me grabbing my arm and pulling me toward the place where the apron sat empty.

Mary covered her gaping mouth with one hand, the other pointed toward the cornhusk doll floating slowly in the current toward the spring pool rock dam. In the clear water under the doll, suspended just over the bottom of the pool I could see the baby's stark white arms and blonde hair moving slowly with the flowing water. I couldn't move or speak, frozen from trying to save the baby. I watched the spring water coming toward my face covering my body, jarring me into doing something. Mary had pushed me, shoved me, to save her master's child. I tried to stand but slipped on the slime-covered rocks lining the spring's bottom and fell deep into the spring pool. My hand touched the baby's dress and I staggered to get a footing and lift the baby girl from the water. The baby fell away turning face up. A white face turned blue with eyes that seemed to stare directly at me, my white face that had caused her to drown.

I climbed from the water and Mary was gone. I could hear her screams from up the hill, she had reached the cabin.

I ran the other way down the steep hill from the spring, crossing the creek at the bottom. I climbed half way up the other side and dropped to the ground gasping for breath. I was choking on the tears and snot filling my mouth. Behind me at the spring pool I could hear a man yell and then the shrieks of the baby's mother.

Minutes later I sneaked back across the branch and up through the trees so I could see the cabin. I looked for Mary.

She lay on the ground beside the smoke house, crying out in short gasps of breath. A man I remembered seeing as he cut wood on the ridge carried the baby's body up the trail and stooped with it in his arms, reaching and yanking Mary's head up. "Look you nigger bitch. You did this! Look goddam you."

Mary cried out, "No! No!"

Another man jerked Mary to her feet, dragging her to a hickory tree. 'Turn around you murdering nigger. Don't want no more "No's" out of your black hide," he yelled. The first man had carried the baby's body into the cabin and came out carrying a rope and a whip. They tied Mary's hands forcing her upright. I tried to get up my courage and go out and tell them it was my fault. I peed my pants at just the thought. Her sack dress was ripped off and she stood naked. Naked against the savage torture. Naked against the words they kept shouting at her. "You drowned the baby. You murdering nigger." The whip fell again and again. Each time the whip lashed the slave girl, she screamed the same words.

"I don't drown no baby. No drown the baby!"

I had to stop her torture. I ran from the woods toward the two men. One saw me and picked up a rock, throwing it and hitting me in the leg. "Get out of here, boy. Don't want no white boy around this naked murdering nigger slave." I felt sure she would tell them it was my fault. My fault for dragging her behind the bramble bush. My fault for causing the baby to drown. A man yelled that she was a murderer and was going to hang for it. They built a fire and stoked it higher. Long into the night they beat the girl. I turned and ran like a coward into the blackness of the night.

Nelson returned the pencil to his pocket and folded the paper tablet he had been writing on. Writing the story came hard, like the memories of what happened at the dogtrot cabin before the war.

The snap of twigs behind him made him turn and look toward the tree line along the ridge. It could have been someone watching, he thought, but they'd already gone. No threat came from the tree line now, but Nelson knew someone had watched him sitting beside Mary's grave. He headed back across the valley to the barn stall he had been sleeping in. The time had come to look for a place of his own in Steelville. The printing press would need a home.

CHAPTER 32

The next morning Nelson told Anne his plans to find a location for his newspaper shop, and then rode the mustang down the hill into the flood torn section of Steelville. He stopped first at the Oliver's to thank them again for taking care of Joshua while they were gone. Mrs. Oliver came out of the partially rebuilt house to greet him.

"I wanted to stop by and thank you both for taking care of the boy," Nelson said, swinging down from the horse.

"That's all right. Mr. Oliver and I would do anything for Miss Anne. Folks here have a lot of respect for her, you know."

"I'm sure she is a fine teacher," Nelson said. "Or did you have something else to say?"

"Yes . . . folks talking about you staying up there . . . going off together and all," Mrs. Oliver said, looking straight at him. "Just what do you intend to do to stop this talk, Mr. Paintier? You said yourself she is a schoolteacher!"

"With people out to kill me, things got a little crazy for both of us. Expect I wouldn't say this so loud she could hear me, but I hope she'll have me for her husband someday soon."

"I hoped you would say that, my boy. Always knew you would turn out to be a fine man and make Anne an honest woman."

With a red flush on his face, Nelson thanked Mrs. Oliver and headed for the remains of the courthouse. Cleanup and rebuilding had been going on there since the flood. The half dozen men working on the building stopped when he rode up.

"Would you like to pitch in and help on the courthouse?" one of the men asked. He was wearing home sewn coveralls and no shirt.

"I would but I'm looking for someone who can help me with county records," Nelson said, walking over and offering his hand and his name.

"Charles Link, county clerk. Some records been coming back, what we found lying along the river banks after the flood. We're drying them best we can. Can't read most of them, ink all washed away."

"Well I'm looking to buy a couple of acres, put up an office and start building a place to live."

"What's your last name, again?" the clerk asked.

"Paintier. Lived here before the war."

"You Levi Paintier's boy?"

"Yes, Levi was my Pa. Lived about quarter mile up to the north of town, before our place burnt."

"I know your place. Squatters were up there for a while, but place is still there. Pay a little tax on it and I think it would be yours again. Damn record's such a mess nobody else could claim it anyway."

"Figure the taxes for me, I'll be back to pay them."

It came as a surprise to Nelson, having a chance to get his home place back, up on the north ridge above town. He left the courthouse and rode up the north hill, along the wagon trail that had first been cut by his father.

The rock chimney and fireplace were hidden by the brush and ivy vines; a closer look showed black soot that covered the chimney and foundation. Charred timbers from the burned house filled the foundation and lay strewn over the rock walls.

He had awakened to see flaming lanterns being thrown through both front windows of the house, the first lantern landed on the bed where his dad slept. His dad sprang from the bed with fire burning all over his body and ran blindly into the cabin wall. Nelson ran toward him, but turned in terror and bolted out the back of the cabin. He watched the riders, from the woods, when they came around the burning cabin. The leader's face burnt into Nelson's memory like the fire burned what remained of his father and their home.

Nelson walked around the charred remains, kicking a few of the burnt timbers back into the foundation walls. He would have to clean up what remained of his home before building anything else on the forty-four acres. Seeing the place where their house had stood made him feel at home again. Riding back to the courthouse, he paid the taxes that were due, and the land was his.

He rode up the south hill to the new home that was being completed for Anne with a renewed spirit believing he could overcome all that faced him. Seeing the burnt-out house convinced him, he could never rest until he faced Spaid. The time had come to hunt him down.

Dyer saw him coming and walked out to meet him.

"Rider came in, Hagan wants to meet tomorrow. Told me where to take you," Dyer said.

"You sure he's not just trying to draw me out?" Nelson said, climbing from his saddle.

He shrugged. "All the men are tired of always being chased or havin' to steal from folks with nothin' left to steal," taking the reins of Nelson's horse.

"Do we need to leave tonight?" Nelson asked.

"It's about half a day's ride so, the mornin's fine."

"Is Anne in the house?" Nelson asked, starting across the front porch of the nearly completed house.

"She walked down into town a while ago, looking for a fiddler."

"A fiddler?"

"Yep, going to have some fiddlin' and singin' to celebrate the new house," Dyer said, leading the horse toward the barn to unsaddle.

"You coming to the celebration, Dyer?"

"You?" Dyer replied.

"Hum . . . " Nelson said.

CHAPTER 33

Dyer shook Nelson awake early the next morning. With a cook fire burning in the back barn lot, Dyer fried up a dozen thick cuts of smoked bacon in a huge cast iron skillet. The four eggs frying in the bacon grease leavings came from the hen's nest Thomas found way in the back of the hayloft.

Thomas stood watching the eggs cook, "That chicken wantin' to go settin' on them eggs. Flogged me all the ways to the front of the hayloft. Went back with the hayfork to gets them."

"That old hen's a mean one," Joshua said.

After a good laugh at Thomas's story and the breakfast under their belt Nelson kissed Anne goodbye and joined Dyer to head south. Dyer took the lead. Nelson felt Anne would be safe while he was away since he had hired two of the local men to help finish the house and to protect her.

Near the Crawford County border Nelson said, "Someone is following us for sure."

"Meetin' place is not far. I'll watch to make sure they don't close on us," Dyer said. "We can pull up over by the cedars."

They didn't have to wait long; Hagan rode up from the south, Red came in behind them.

Hagan rode his horse right against the side of Nelson's mustang, "Time there I wanted to kill both you and your woman," Hagan said, having to turn his horse to avoid the mustang's back feet about to come his way.

"She shot him, because she knew I was going to," Nelson said, riding back to the side of Hagan's horse.

"Kinda thought you might try that," Hagan said. "Surprised the hell out of me when the schoolteacher shot him. She saved your life, mister."

"You did ask me here to talk about the pardons, right?" Nelson asked, backing away from Hagan and swinging from the saddle to the ground. He stood with his back to a cedar.

"Sonofabitch Turner is dead as he can be, so is my boy. Get on with it." Finding a fallen log they both sat looking at each other.

"Pardons would be for all your men, raiding would have to stop when they sign them," Nelson said.

"Only a couple of them say they ain't signin' nothin'. Rest are ready to quit this kind of life, go back home."

"You say where and when we can meet and I'll bring the pardons to sign."

"Who signs for the army?" Hagan asked.

"After you and your men sign, the pardons go to the commander at Jefferson Barracks to sign."

"I have to see him sign. Ain't going to put my trust in that happening down the road a piece," Hagan said, shaking his head side to side.

"All of you go in ridin' up to the fort would create quite a stir. Done some crazier things for you though."

"If that's the way it has to be, tell me when to meet you. Be on the edge of the timber outside Saint Louis. Anybody tries to spring a trap on us, gonna be a lot of dead people," said Hagan.

"I'll meet you at the Meramec River outside of Saint Louis. One week from today, if that's not too soon for you to round up your boys," Nelson said.

With the agreement reached, Hagan and Red headed west at a fast gallop, Nelson looked at Dyer asking for his opinion on the negotiations just completed.

"Looking for my opinion, are you?" Dyer asked. "Takin' that bunch into Jefferson Barracks be like dancing barefoot on a rattlesnake."

"Going to lead them in there. If they keep that damn black flag in their saddlebags it should be okay. Command will be jarred up some."

"Let's get back to Steelville. Fiddler be coming tonight, along with half the curious town folks," Dyer said.

"Expect most of them like to hear some good fiddling music. Cheer them up after the flood and all they have been through," Nelson said.

CHAPTER 34

Four lamps were struck and lighting the front porch of the new house when folks began to arrive. The strains of Old Joe Tucker from Fiddlin' Tom's gut-strung Ozark fiddle could be heard clear across the Steelville valley. Anne set out the cookies and pies she had baked for the folks to eat. Being a schoolteacher she had made sweet tea for them to drink instead of hard liquor. She stood at the door of the house.

"House is open, come on through, glad to have you," she said to the visitors.

Nelson and Dyer stood in the door of the barn and kept an eye on who came up the hill. The smell of Anne's apple pies as they came out of the oven had them walking down the hill to the front porch.

"Well hello, Mr. Paintier and Mr. Spencer," Anne quipped, making a sweeping bow and motioning for them to join her for a look at the inside of the new house.

"Howdy, Miss Anne. House is looking mighty fine, apple pie smell catches a man's nose and don't want to let go," Nelson said.

"Okay, boys. I understand what you're wanting. Sit down on the edge of the porch and let's see what I can come up with," Anne said. "Both you boys are going to have to do a little jig to a fiddle tune, before you get any pie."

Dyer went first, hitting a solid lick with his foot behind and across the back of his knee. The fiddler must have liked the jigging; he bowed up the tempo faster and faster.

"Didn't know you had jig stepping hiding in there," Anne said.

"Don't get to come out much, with the life I been leadin'," Dyer said, dropping to the porch out of breath.

"Now it's your turn, Mr. Paintier," reaching to pull Nelson to his feet.

"Fiddlin' Tom, how about 'Mary of The Wild Moor'," Nelson asked.

"Sorry, don't know that one, but here's a little waltz been playing since I was a boy," Fiddlin' Tom said, cutting into about the most beautiful waltz Nelson had ever heard.

"Dance with me, Miss Ruth Anne," Nelson said, bowing before taking a firm grip on her waist and turning with her to the one-two-three beat of the waltz.

"You're quite a dancing man, Mr. Paintier. You're going to have all those town folk standing there, staring at us and talking about me for a month you know."

"I know, Anne," Nelson said, pulling her closer, "Something I want to say real bad right now. Like how much I love you and I know it's a strange place to ask. Marry me, Anne."

She didn't need to answer, instead Nelson got kissed like never before, right there on the porch, stepping one-two-three to a waltz he didn't even know the name of. *I guess she said yes.*

Nelson waltzed Anne to the side of Fiddlin' Tom. The music trailed off on a squeak from the e string of the fiddle. Tom got the news first-hand from Nelson. His next note came right from the *"Wedding March"*. Dyer and Joshua stood up, giving Anne and Nelson a what-just-happened look. Joshua started clapping first, then the circle of Steelville folks listening to the music joined in. Nelson saw the big smile on Mrs. Oliver's face and then the beaming coming from Anne's.

"You know, you might end up being sorry about marrying a school teacher," Anne said, still turning with him to the fiddle music.

"Never, since the school teacher is you."

"Folks expect more from a teacher. Helping with church, and town things."

"Good. We can both help."

"All right then. After all that, I best tell you. Yes, I'll marry you, Captain Paintier!"

CHAPTER 35

The porch lamps had cooled and were stored away when Nelson left Anne and her new house to return to his bed in the horse barn. He walked up the hill, thinking of Anne and how she had accepted him to be her husband. He had realized the first time they met, he wanted her for all of his life. The clear night and full moon caused him to pause and turn back toward the house and Anne. Stopping, he heard horses and riders come over the ridge. They were shooting at the barn and him too, before they even got close. Dyer came out of the barn carrying two rifles; he threw one to Nelson and started firing the other at the oncoming riders.

"Who the hell is this?" Dyer shouted.

"Get inside, before we both get shot," Nelson said, running past Dyer into the barn.

Dyer followed, joining Nelson behind a heavy stall wall.

"Keep some fire on them from here. I'm going out the back and get to Anne and the house," Nelson said, as he headed for the back of the barn. When the back door swung open, he got nicked in the face by flying wood chips.

"Damn, Dyer, they got us pinned in here," Nelson yelled, setting up to guard the back of the barn.

"Couple of them behind the rock wall across the road. Easy to keep us pinned in here till morning," Dyer said.

"If you see them move down the hill toward Anne and Joshua, I'm going to have to break out of here," Nelson said, shooting at a moving shadow behind the barn. Nelson heard a groan from the man he shot at and saw him crawl to the other side of the garden.

"Dyer, they're after you, they're after me. Must be Spaid's men that have been running guns for the old judge from Crawford County."

"What the hell did you do to have them want to kill you?" Dyer said, glancing two shots off the top of the rock wall, above the head of one of the shooters.

"Long story, more about what I'm going to do. They're coming again, don't let them get in the barn."

"Got two coming up here," Dyer said, reloading his carbine.

Two shotgun blasts fired from behind the men running at the barn dropped them to their knees. The men turned around to fire at where the shots were coming from, only to see the burning powder from half a dozen other pistols and shotguns.

"Looks like a couple of them are backing off here. We got a lot of help from somebody," Dyer said.

"Leaving faster than they came," Nelson said. "Who drove them off?"

"You okay in there, boys?" The voice came from one of the men crossing the rock wall headed for the barn.

"We're fine," Dyer said, stepping into the road.

"Mr. Oliver, who all's with you?" Nelson asked. "Riders surprised us, got the drop on us when we headed back from the new house."

"Mr. Gunther thought something was up. Saw them circle up on the road when the fiddler finished playing," Mr. Oliver said. "Came got me, rest of the folks came too."

"Mighty grateful to all you folks," Nelson said, catching a glance of Anne just before she grabbed him around the waist.

"Is this ever going to stop?" Anne pleaded.

"Oh, it's going to stop and soon. Next week Hagan and his men are riding into Saint Louis with me and the pardons will be signed. Then I'm coming back here and tracking down Spaid to end this."

"The town folks coming out to help you says a lot," Anne said.

"Might have something to do with their school teacher up here where all this shooting's going on. Don't you think?" Nelson asked.

With a few days left before he planned to leave for Saint Louis, Nelson hired three men to help him start cleaning up his dad's house across the valley. With the charred remains of the timbers and all the rock foundations removed, Nelson staked out the location for his print shop, and drew plans for a two-bedroom house, he would ask Anne to live in as his wife.

Finished with the first steps in building the shop and house, he needed to get ready for the trip to Saint Louis. He got out the captain's uniform he had been carrying in his saddlebags and brushed it clean. He and Dyer would leave in the morning.

Both men were awake at daybreak and ready to travel. Nelson had carefully folded the uniform to keep it neat for the ride to the Jefferson Barracks Post.

When they reached a stand of heavy timber a few miles from the Meramec River meeting place, the first two of Hagan's men reined their horses out of the cover of the trees to join them.

"Didn't see any sign of you or your horses before you rode up," Nelson said, but the men didn't answer.

"They learn to hide in the trees if they want to stay alive," Dyer said.

At the end of the next mile, Nelson and Dyer had eighteen riders along with Hagan and Red with them. They formed up four abreast through the south edges of Saint Louis.

"Going to stop about now and put on that uniform?" Dyer asked.

"Thought about wearing it, again. Something just wrong about doing that after shooting the federal soldier when we got ambushed."

"I wondered if that still bothered you," Dyer said.

"Don't plan to wear Yankee Blue ever again. I'll ride in there looking more like the men alongside us."

Hagan rode up to the side of Nelson's horse.

"Nelson, you realize if this gets messed up today, going to be a lot of Yankees die. My men are carrying five to six firearms each and they aim to empty them all before it ends."

"I understand, Hagan. Ask them to keep the pistols out of sight. There's going to be some excitement when they realize who's coming through the front gate of the fort, don't know how this will set with the federals. Keep everybody calm."

The closer they got to Jefferson Barracks the more of a stir they were causing. The soldiers in blue they passed saw men dressed like they had been on a thousand mile ride, unshaven, long beards draped down over their chests. Each wore a dark coat long enough to cover the weapons they carried.

One of the troops of mounted soldiers they passed redirected two of their riders; sending them at a gallop toward the fort.

"They're going to be a welcoming committee now, I'm thinkin'," Hagan said.

"Gates open up ahead. Follow my lead, ride right in there. Stay formed up behind me," Nelson said.

"Ride proud, boys," Hagan said.

Through the gates of Jefferson Barracks, Captain Nelson Paintier led the band of notorious bushwhackers, each of Hagan's men trusting Paintier, not for what he had said, but for the deeds they had seen him do.

When Paintier lifted his hand to stop in the middle of the fort's parade ground, Hagan's men broke the four-man formation and formed a circle with their horses, each rider facing outward protecting each other's back.

The troops standing at attention on the side of the parade ground came toward the circle with bayonets mounted. They formed a circle around the riders, each taking aim at the bushwhacker in front.

At the first sight of the bayonets, Hagan's men drew a pistol to each hand and leveled them at the soldiers that would be the first to die.

"Hold it, Damn it," shouted the powerful voice from the steps of the command barracks. "Paintier! You wantin' to die, bringin' those men in here?"

"All of them came to see you sign the pardons you sent me with, General," said Captain Nelson Paintier.

"Troop commanders, have your men lower their weapons," the General said.

"Put them away, boys," Hagan said.

"I am going to guess that's Hagan and his men you are riding with, Captain Paintier."

"Correct, sir," saluting the general.

"Dismount, Paintier, bring him in."

Hagan followed Nelson up the steps; his men held the circle, unbroken, weapons stowed.

The General stood behind his desk, facing Hagan, "I was sorry to hear what happened to your boy, Hagan."

Hagan didn't respond. The General looked at Nelson, "I'm not going to ask what happened to Turner. Guessin' I won't have to deal with him. Correct, Captain?"

"Correct, sir."

Each of Hagan's men took their turn to sign a pardon. Some could only make X'es while others wrote out their names in crude broken letters. Nelson watched, making sure each man's name or mark got written on a pardon. Hagan signed last, followed by the General of the Western Territory.

"Hagan, this pardon is unconditional and allows your men to leave here carrying their weapons. I am sending Captain Paintier back to southern Missouri with you. I'm holding your discharge, Paintier, until the raiding settles down. Ride home and keep track of these fellows. Any raiding, and I'll send in my troops to stop it. You stay, Captain Paintier. I need to talk to you about another matter. Good luck, Mr. Hagan."

Hagan left the pardon signing and joined his men in the parade ground of the fort.

"Paintier, we captured a wagon of small arms headed south out of Jefferson City last week. Got the team driver to talk and found out they were headed for a meet with Confederate scouts, still wanting to keep fighting, down on the Arkansas border," said the General. "They wouldn't tell us who was backing the enterprise, but we've been watching a senator in the state government for some time now."

"That man happen to be from Steelville?" Nelson asked.

"Thought you might have an idea or two on this, Paintier. We lost one of our agents in Jefferson City a few weeks ago, shot in the head. He'd sent a telegram night he was killed, so we knew you were connected somehow."

"Yes, sir. He'd been to see me in the middle of the night. Saw them carry him up out of the river the next morning."

"Keep an eye out, Paintier. Pass along anything you find out. Good work with the pardons," The General said, stepping around the desk and shaking Nelson's hand. "Thank you soldier."

Hagan and Dyer stood with the horses, waiting for Nelson. The other men had left the fort for home. Nelson felt the three of them probably could use a stop in Saint Louis for a drink before making the ride home.

"Head up into Saint Louis? Lift a couple before heading to Steelville?" Nelson asked. I have a little business to attend to before heading home.

Dyer turned his horse, "I'm heading on for Steelville. Promised Anne to help with the last work on the house."

He didn't have to ask Hagan twice, they rode out of the fort and into Saint Louis. After the stop at the tavern, Nelson made one other stop in Saint Louis at the shipping company and then headed home, with Hagan at his side.

CHAPTER 36

"What's your plan, Hagan? Staying around Rolla or Springfield?" Nelson asked.

"I rustled a lot of people around both of those places. Some are gonna want payback from me. Understand their feelin's, but I won't be able to sit still for any payback," Hagan said.

"I've got some work, if you feel like staying for a while to help. Starting a newspaper in Steelville. Got plans for a printing shop building that's got to go up first," Nelson said while they crossed a low water crossing on the Meramec River.

"Broke as hell, me and all the boys. Never did have much more than something to eat. Some days not even that," Hagan said, stopping to let his horse drink. "Could stay around for a while; bring in a couple of the boys to help build your shop. Bunch of them live close to Steelville."

"You notice anything about the bunch passed us just before the river?" Nelson asked.

"One of them took a lot of notice of you. Turned in the saddle after they passed."

"Just someone I thought I'd seen before," Nelson said, "Let's head on out, see if we can't put some distance between them and us."

Thirty miles out from Steelville Nelson asked, "Hagan, mind riding ahead? Somebody is following us, got that feeling they are about a mile or so back."

"Staying together be better. We can just fade into the timber, see who comes up."

"Lead away, mister," Nelson said.

Hagan pulled up on a ridge south of the trace, "Get a look from here, and see what they are up to."

"I hear them coming hard now. Lost sight of us on the trace," Nelson said.

The six riders rode right on past where Hagan and Nelson had left the trace. Nelson heard them stop and turn back; they had met three more men that had been coming from the west.

"They're going to find where we turned off soon," Hagan said, "Let's go, keep up."

Nelson didn't know where Hagan would lead, but he realized with nine men chasing them, Hagan would get them to a spot where they could at least hold the riders off.

"Big . . . cave . . . couple miles ahead. If they follow we can put up quite a fight from inside," Hagan said.

Hagan and Nelson rode right into the mouth of the huge cavern, taking their horses around several turns and tying them in safety. Back at the mouth of the cave Hagan motioned Nelson to a rock wall.

"Piled that wall up about a year back. Never knew I would be behind it with a Yankee," Hagan said.

"Glad you are."

During the next few minutes while they waited for the men chasing them, Nelson explained to Hagan that a state senator's henchman had killed a federal agent to protect their gunrunning and the ex sheriff had also been ordered to kill him.

Both of them heard the riders cross between the cave and the Meramec River. The riders fanned out outside of the cave and started firing into the cave's darkness.

"Save your lead, Nelson. They might keep us in here for quite a while. Plenty of water back in the cave."

196

"Bet they'll going to come charging up here after dark," Nelson said.

"They will. We can hold off an army behind this wall. They aren't likely to come all at once. Send a couple fools up first. Let them get close."

Twice in the late afternoon, Spaid and his men tested Nelson and Hagan's firepower with a burst of rifle fire and a move to get closer to the mouth of the cave. Nelson and Hagan returned fire and heard two of the men shout to Spaid they had been hit. As soon as darkness came, Nelson watched the flickering of a torch being lit off to the side of the cave. The man stayed out of sight, but managed to fling the lit torch into the cave behind him.

"The bastards are trying to backlight us," Nelson said.

"If he tries that again I'm going to move over to the side and drop him. That'll keep them from sneaking up on the side of the cave," Hagan said, moving past the rock wall and into a shallow rock depression that ran across the mouth of the cave. The next man carrying a torch died with it still in his hands. Hagan's shot knocked him backward onto the burning torch. The attacks slowed down after the torch throwing.

"I'll keep a watch on them, if you want to slip back and bring up some water to drink," Nelson said.

"I don't think they're going to try and rush us again tonight. They might have to try and starve us out," Hagan said heading into the large cavern behind them.

The next afternoon Nelson realized Hagan may have been right about them being starved out. Only a shot or two came from the men along the river all day. They were settled in for a long stay out there.

The third day brought only light firing to keep Nelson and Hagan pinned in the cave.

"This is getting old, Hagan. Think we should try and ride out of here?"

"Good way to get killed, I think. Hang on, things could change soon out there," Hagan said.

The fourth morning's dawn came with a downpour. From inside the cave both men watched the riders, moving about trying to get shelter from the rain.

"Chance to drop a couple out there; they're getting careless it looks like," Nelson said.

"You're right, likely get one before they drop out of sight in the brush." Hagan said, sitting more relaxed than Nelson ever could.

The rain had started to let up when both of them heard the firing start up outside. No lead was coming their way.

"Took them longer to get here than I expected," Hagan said.

"Who? Your men?" Nelson asked.

"Yep, they watch out for me. Knew if I didn't show up in Steelville, some of them would come looking. Probably been watching what's going on out there for a few hours."

"Come on, let's give them a hand," Nelson said, leaving the rock wall and joining the push to drive off Spaid's men.

Six of Hagan's men riding from the east attacked the rain soaked men. All six carried a pistol in each hand, firing them until empty and gripping another two from their belt to continue pumping lead at the riders. Hagan's men had the riders beat, the two who were left rode for their lives.

"Hey, Red, glad you came along," Hagan said. "Things were starting to look grim for us in there."

"Sorry, boss couple of those men got away, rest of them look mighty dead."

"Spaid's gone, got away," Nelson said, After he had a chance to look over the bodies for a familiar face.

"Want us to go after him?" Red asked.

"This is one score I'm going to have to settle on my own. Spaid must be one of the ones, got away; the bastard burned my dad alive about fifteen years ago," Nelson said, heading for his horse.

CHAPTER 37

Their trail led north from the Meramec River. Nelson pushed the roan hard. Their tracks showed the men had ridden at a gallop for the first few miles, and then slowed. They may have thought no one would follow after the fight on the Meramec River ended. Nelson had connected with his spurs twice and the big horse answered the call stretching the gallop. The soggy road hadn't filled the deep tracks with water yet, he knew the men were just ahead.

"Come on horse, show a little more of your mustang spirit and we will have those bastards in our sights."

Now he saw them, turning in their saddles to see who had followed them. They didn't run, just turned their horses and moved apart about eight feet, giving Nelson two targets to shoot at instead of one. He pulled the roan up hard, before starting ahead at a slow walk, the men had their pistols drawn and they started toward him at a gallop.

Bushwhacker tactics came naturally to Nelson now, he had been taught well. He charged with a pistol in each hand, holding the horse's reins in his mouth.

They started firing before he did, luckily they were wild shots. One came close enough, Nelson heard the snap of it passing his right ear. He responded by blowing the man out of the saddle. The fellow about to pass him on his right was luckier, Nelson's shot hit his left arm, the big .44 slug knocked him backward out of the saddle. Nelson turned his horse and rode back to where the man had fallen in the mud.

"Where's Spaid, holed up damn it?" Nelson demanded.

"Fuck you, Yankee shit," the wounded man said, trying to sit up in the mud.

Nelson dropped from the saddle and kicked the man's pistol away. He set his boot hard into the wounded man's chest, the mud oozed up around both of his ears.

"Going to ask you again, where do I find Spaid?"

"Spaid's going to kill you for this."

After that reply, Nelson left the man and went to his saddlebag, returning with heavy rope. He made a loop and dropped it around the man's neck.

"Doesn't matter to me, you want to die here like your friend over there?" Nelson said, drawing the loop tight and tossing the end of the rope over an overhanging limb.

"Tying this to my saddle horn, and not even going to look back at what happens to your neck."

The man didn't say any more up until the time Nelson turned the mustang north and yanked him to his feet.

"Stop! He . . . rode . . . away last night. Thought we would kill you for sure."

"Well, he was damn wrong, wasn't he? Where's he staying?"

"Place of his down—loosen the damn rope. On the Osage River near Vienna."

"I'm going to let you go. Put you back on that horse. I want you to tell Spaid, Paintier is coming for him. Hear that?"

The man rode slumped in the saddle, headed to the north at a slow walk. Nelson didn't waste time, he reined the horse back south to the Saint Louis-Rolla trace. He wanted to get back to Anne.

He found her later that day, at the new house.

"Dyer thought you would be coming soon. I was so worried," Anne said. "Hagan came through here two hours ago. Told us what happened at the cave."

"Thought I had Spaid in my sights, ended up shooting two of his men. He got away during the night before Hagan's men got there."

"Clean up at the water tank and I'll fix you something to eat," Anne said, finally letting go of the hug she had planted around him when he arrived.

"Be right in," Nelson said, kissing Anne on the lips.

After he watered his horse and dropped some hay from the loft, he stopped to talk to Thomas, who was planting in the garden. Thomas got up from his knees and set down the bag of seeds he had been planting.

"Think any of those seeds will sprout, up here in red clay, Thomas?"

"Yes, sir, they gonna grow. Went way out back there and got some buckets of that old horse manure, mixed it all in with this here clay. They's gonna grow all right."

"I'm going to start work soon on a place over across the valley. I'd like to have your help over there."

"Be proud to help you, Mr. Nelson," Thomas said.

"I will have a place for you to live in the shop when it is finished."

"Up on the other ridge, sir?"

"Yes, years ago my dad and I lived up there. House got burned down."

"Walked up there before, saw you sitting alongside that pile of rock. Didn't wanna bother you, writin' on that paper."

"It's just some words, Thomas. About a little slave girl. She is buried up there under those rocks. Her name was Mary."

"Can you show me some of them words?"

"Yes. You have a good teacher here with Miss Anne. She can teach you to read those words. She wants to help you a little each day." Looking at the old black man Nelson asked, "Thomas, you seem so sad. What is it?"

"Slaves way back 'fore the war talked about a nigger girl. Men caught her and hung her, right here in this town, you toles me. Is that her grave, up yonder on the bluff?"

"It is, Thomas. My words are about her."

"Thank you, Mr. Nelson, for telling me."

"The story is not quite finished, I'll read it to you sometime soon."

Nelson left as the old man got back on his knees, carefully dropping the sweet corn seeds and covering them with a slow sweep of his hand. The corn would grow, Thomas had made sure. The smell of frying bacon and eggs cooking got his attention; Damn, I'm hungry, he thought.

"Thomas is going to have the sweet corn coming up tomorrow," Nelson kidded Anne as he went into the kitchen, "Richened up the soil a bit."

"Sit there, Mister. I'll have your plate ready real soon," Anne said.

"Can you talk and cook?" Nelson asked.

"Sure, if you want burnt eggs with cracklings instead of bacon."

"Oh!"

CHAPTER 38

After breakfast Anne called for a showdown, "Nelson, why don't you take Hagan and go finish Spaid?" she said standing behind Nelson with her hands on his shoulders.

"Hagan's men saved us on the Meramec, but I've got to finish this fight with Spaid on my own."

"Are you sure you know why Spaid's out to kill you?"

"Spaid's working for the senator who's going to run for governor. The senator doesn't want the things I know about him to be published."

"Must be more than that. Just a book?" Anne asked.

"Even a few words can change history," Nelson said, "but I think it's got to be more about Spaid's men who killed the federal agent in Jefferson City. If word got out about his gun-running support for the Confederate troops turned bushwhackers it would ruin him for sure."

"Rest a few days. I would like to know more about my husband to be."

"And what would you like to know about this worn out old soldier?"

"Oh, I want to know about your father, about the dogtrot cabin you lived in up on the trace, and just where is it, you are going to move me to?"

"Tomorrow I'll take you across the valley to the place where my father's house stood and show you the land where we can build our home."

With a good night's rest under his belt he and Anne walked down the hill and waded Yadkin Creek. On the other side, Anne took him a quarter mile downstream to the place where her sister's home had stood.

"That night, the creek was running full when everyone went to bed. I remember hearing thunder and rain—Rain coming down so hard, like I can't ever remember."

"I'd rode through a lot of it, that night on the way here," Nelson said.

"It had to be a wall of water, ripped right through the store and court house building. Took the houses from both sides of the creek. I ran down to warn them, the rushing water almost got me. I was too late."

"Nothing you could do. Water tore the houses right off the foundations. Good thing Joshua and his mother were sleeping upstairs when it came."

"Still feels like it was my fault, I didn't go sooner," Anne said.

"You are not to blame for your sister's drowning. Tell me what was she like?"

"She had a hard time with Dyer being gone, riding with the bushwhackers and all. She always did her best to protect Joshua. Saw her chase a gang of boys off with a club that were tormenting him about his dad. When she would start to drink Joshua would come over and stay with me. Got to the point she was drunk more often than not. I think she just gave up."

"She tried her best, out there on the roof, to save Joshua. She didn't see the limb coming that caught her up. Threw her into the currents. She was gone so quick. I might not have gotten out of the flood if it wasn't for her screaming for help on their house roof."

"Come on, no more sad talk. Show me the land. Take my hand, lead the way, Mr. Paintier."

They climbed the north side of the valley, past the church where Nelson had found his father's grave, and up the hill to the land where he wanted their house to be built.

"We lived there, right in the stand of trees. They came in the night, throwing flaming lanterns in on us. Then the shooting started. They weren't watching the back of the house. I ran through the trees and back into town to hide. They hanged Mary the next morning."

"You stayed and didn't leave Steelville right away?"

"Stayed for the girl. I was the only friend she had. Hid out with the crowd out in front of the gallows until they covered her face."

"Did she see you, there in the crowd?"

"Her eyes were open wide with fright. She saw me. Those staring eyes asking why didn't you tell them, why didn't you save me," Nelson said. "Her face has haunted me."

"Nelson, you did all you could. Your book will tell what really happened at the spring pool. I'll help you."

"I need to finish it, write the last chapter here, just down the hill where she is buried. Take it to Saint Louis to a friend in the printing business that's waiting to publish it. Then I can start work on the newspaper."

"What do we need to print the newspaper?" Anne asked.

"Printing press is coming by steamship soon. Scheduled to be delivered in Jefferson City. That's never going to happen with Spaid and the senator watching. Ship will have to stop at Hermann for the ironworks deliveries, so I'll have an ore wagon and team up there to pick it up."

Nelson and Anne walked over the forty-acre tract and talked about where Anne wanted their house to be built. She liked an open area near to the corner of the land facing the valley and Nelson agreed. With their home location planned, they crossed the valley, to talk with Dyer about getting carpenters to start building.

"I need to go to the ironworks sawmill tomorrow, Anne. Would you like to go? We can stop by the dogtrot cabin for you to see what we built years ago."

As they continued to walk, Anne asked, "Have you thought about Spaid and his men? Maybe an ambush?"

"Dyer is going to ride out ahead of us to be sure it's safe. He wants to get supplies at the Works anyway. If you don't mind, I'd like to head up the creek hollow and see Spaid's sister on the way."

"Does she know where her brother's place is up on the Osage?" Anne asked.

"I don't know, but she told me she knew enough about things he'd done for him to kill her. I want to see if she'll tell me what she knows."

CHAPTER 39

Driving a team of fine mules and a wagon Anne borrowed from the Olivers, Nelson and Anne started up the valley toward Jenny Spaid's cabin. Nelson's roan gelding trotted along tied behind. Less than halfway to the cabin they saw Jenny's sow and litter. The hog stopped in front of them and lifted its nose, grunting loudly.

"Sow's ranging a long way for food," Anne said.

"It's strange the pigs are this far from the cabin. Jenny had them penned up close when I came up here the first time."

"They must have found a hole in the fence," Anne said.

"I need to get on up to Jenny's cabin, see what might be going on," Nelson said, climbing down from the wagon and untying his horse from the rear of the wagon.

As he got closer to the cabin, Nelson saw the rails around the hog pen had been broken, and the front door to the cabin stood open. Nelson called out for the old woman, and then went to see if she was inside the cabin. When he came out Anne had the team of mules tied to the broken fence.

"She's not here, Anne. Check the shed out back, I'll go through the cabin again."

"Not back here, either," shouted Anne.

"No one inside, all torn up like somebody was looking for something," Nelson said, stepping out the back of the cabin.

"The root cellar back there has been cleaned out," Anne said.

"She's gone. He must have taken her. Tried to make it look like raiders did it. Told me she had written down enough about Spaid to get him hung."

"Where would she hide something like that?" Anne asked.

"She's a stubborn old gal, she would never tell Spaid where she hid her writings."

"I'll start searching in the shed," Anne said.

"I'll go through the cabin, I really doubt if they found where she hid her papers," Nelson said, heading back into the cabin.

Nelson climbed on a chair and searched high in the broken chinking between the logs. He found plenty of cow dung that had been used to plug holes, but no papers. After two hours of searching, he pulled the chairs up to the table and sat with Anne to think.

"When I came to see her the first time . . . something she said . . . about the papers she had written. She told me 'Gonna be a cold spring before he finds them.' We have to find the spring. There has to be a spring for drinking water, back on the hillside."

"There should be a heavy path where she walks to get water," Anne said, leaving the cabin and walking around to the back. "Here," pointing toward the path.

In less than a hundred yards up the valley, they found the rock-wall spring. Nelson opened the wooden cover and reached to feel around the back wall, "She's got a jar tied up way in the back." Nelson tried to pull the jug out.

"Hand it to me, if you can reach it," Anne said.

"Can't, it's tied by a cord up through the back wall. See if you can cut it loose from up back. Here, take my knife."

Anne climbed over the back of the spring and cut the cord holding the jug.

"Got it," Nelson said as he lifted the jug from the spring water and handed it to Anne.

"Lordy, the top is tight. Sides all covered with some kind of slime," Anne said.

"Let me see if I can get it open," Nelson tapped the edge of the jug top with his knife, "There, the top's coming off."

Spaid's history of murder and robbery fell to the ground at Nelson and Anne's feet. Scraps of paper, each with place, dates, and crimes. Nelson knelt and picked up the papers, unrolling each, and stopping to read the faint pencil marking on them.

"My God, Anne. Spaid did things that got blamed on Hagan and his men. Even some of the robberies everyone thought Bloody Bill Anderson had done."

"Do you think Spaid took her, to stop her from telling what she knows?"

"From what she told me he knew she had written it all down. Either he took her, or she got away, and hid in the hills. He'll be back here soon, Anne."

"We need to get out of here, go get help," Anne tugged at his arm.

"You need to go, Anne. Don't send help, it might just scare him off. He'll be by himself if he comes. His men all got shot up back on the Meramec. Go now, Anne. Take the team and wagon back to Steelville."

With Anne on the way to safety, Nelson stuffed the faded scraps of paper spelling out Spaid's crimes into his saddlebags before he led his horse up the valley out of sight of the cabin, and tied it to a stout tree limb. Walking back, he tried to think out a plan for when Sheriff Spaid showed up.

Best to just shoot the son-of-a-bitch, rather than ask why. Why he had burned down their house and killed Nelson's father. Back at the cabin, he picked a spot just off to the side of the cast iron cook stove to wait.

Less than an hour had passed when Spaid arrived, "Come out here, Paintier."

"Stay . . . there, Nelson." He heard Anne's muffled voice.

Nelson bolted out the door of the cabin to find Spaid sitting with Anne in front of him on his horse.

"Look what I found coming out of the valley, Paintier," Spaid said, sliding off the side of his horse and pulling Anne with him, his pistol pointed at her neck.

"Let her go, Spaid. This fight is between you and me." Nelson stepped through the open doorway with his .44 in his hand.

"Where's that old bitch sister of mine, Paintier?"

"I guess she knew you were coming back and left, Spaid," Nelson said, holding his pistol pointed at the floor.

"Get back in the cabin." Spaid said, as he pushed Anne forward and forced Nelson into the cabin door.

"Let her go, Spaid."

"Throw that cannon you're holding over in the corner, Paintier, and I'll let her go."

With no option left, Nelson tossed his .44 into the back corner of the cabin.

"Let me go, you scum," Anne said sinking her boot heel into Spaid's foot.

"You whore," he hit Anne in the side of the head with his pistol. She fell to the cabin floor at his feet.

"You're going to die for that, Spaid," Nelson said.

"It's funny you saying that, standing there empty handed," Spaid cocked the hammer and leveled his pistol at Nelson, "Should have gotten this done years ago."

The explosion came from behind Spaid. Smoke filled the doorway and swept around the sheriff. Nelson dove across the floor, sliding into the corner to grab the .44. His shot hit Spaid square in the chest, knocking him right through the cabin door. Spaid fell dead right at the feet of a powder-covered old woman, still holding what was left of her exploded blunderbuss and trying to wipe her eyes.

"Throwing that revolver into the corner wasn't the smartest thing you ever did, boy," Jenny Spaid, said as she stepped across her dead brothers face.

After Nelson got over the shock of seeing Jenny he rushed to lift Anne's head from the floor.

"I'll get some spring water for her face, that'll get her goin'," Jenny Spaid said, heading around the cabin.

"Had a feeling you might be around somewhere," shouted Nelson. "Lucky for us you hadn't been scared too far off."

Jenny Spaid quickly returned and poured most of the ladle of spring water over Anne's face. With the rest she wet her sleeve to wipe the gunpowder off her face.

"Anne, wake up," Nelson used his hand to get the water off her face.

Her eyes opened and she struggled to sit up. "Wh . . . what happened?"

"Jenny Spaid sneaked up and tried to shoot her brother," Nelson said.

"Jenny, where had you been?" asked Anne.

"Been hiding up on the mountain all along. Just waiting for him to come back," said Jenny Spaid.

"The old gun exploded in her face. Scared Spaid so bad he turned around to face her, gave me time to kill him.

Anne gripped his arms and pulled them around her, "I thought . . . he was . . . going to kill you."

"So did I," Nelson said, holding her close.

CHAPTER 40

Laying the first sheet of paper in the printing press, Nelson struck the front page of his newspaper. The news had come direct to him, by messenger, from the commanding general of Jefferson Barracks.

State Senator Saunders Arrested for Murder
Former Judge of Crawford County has been arrested by federal agents for the murder of agent Edwin Conway in April of this year.

After he had penned and set the print for the articles to be in the first issue of The Crawford County Journal, Nelson spent several days on the bluff above Steelville working to finish the story of *"Mary, the Slave Girl."*

With the manuscript in his hand, Nelson asked Thomas to go with him to Mary's grave. Together they climbed the steep pathway to the top of the bluff.

"Sit here beside me, Thomas. I know you can't read all the words of Mary's story yet. So I would like to read it to you."

"Thank you, sir," Thomas said.

Nelson unfolded his writings and read Thomas the story of Mary. Thomas didn't speak or stand while Nelson read Mary's story. At the end Nelson looked away as Thomas wiped the tears that stained his face. They sat, quiet without speaking for some time. Finally Nelson spoke, "Thomas, you never told me why you came to the Iron Works and the dogtrot cabin. Were you looking for someone there?" Nelson asked.

"I'se tole . . . you, sir, about spirits that came upon me. Feels like it might be the spirit of my little Mary girl, master took away. Feel that same spirit here by this pile of rocks. Them rocks sitting on this slave girl."

"I guess we will never know whose child lies here. But the people still left who hanged her will know she didn't drown the baby," Nelson said. "Walk back with me, Thomas?"

"No, sir . . . if it's all right I like to stay here for a bit," Thomas said.

Nelson laid his hand on the old man's back, gently touched him, and then quietly turned away.

***

With five wagonloads of lumber stacked by the print shop, work had started on the home for Anne. Leaving a fine master carpenter in charge, Nelson crossed the valley to meet Anne. News had come, the traveling preacher would be in Steelville that morning. Nelson and Anne were going to the courthouse for a wedding certificate before meeting the preacher at the church.

"Are you ready for this?" Nelson asked in a most serious manner.

"I've got the chickens fed and breakfast on the table for Joshua," Anne said with a smile.

"I don't mean, ready for today. Are you ready for a lifetime with Nelson Paintier?"

"Shut up, Captain. Come on, we're getting married today," Anne said.

Author's Notes and Thank You to those who were so much help in the writing of this Novel.

To Dr. Pfister, Your Introduction to The Hawksbill Crag paints Civil War History with a wide brush of knowledge, providing the perfect setting for this story. Like the set designer for a movie, your written pictures propel the reader forward to join Captain Nelson Paintier as he takes his historic journey home to find redemption and to help cement the bonds for a United States of America.

To Diana Ross, a fine copy editor who stuck with me and continued to edit as I continued to rewrite.

To RoxAnne, my wife and horse lover companion for 30 years, thank you for listening each evening as I told of Paintier's struggles in bushwhacker ravaged Southern Missouri. Readers will feel and appreciate your love of horses that found its way into this story of a man and the horses that carry him through the guerrilla territory of Civil War southern Missouri and Arkansas.

To Derrald Farnsworth-Livingston for taking the beautiful photograph of The Hawksbill Crag, on the morning when the lighting was perfect. Visit his website to purchase prints of this and other photographs of the Ozarks.

To Connie Luebbert of the Salt and Light Studios, Columbia, Missouri for finding the time to design a smashingly great cover for the novel. Her graphic art work is getting international attention. Great job Connie.

ABOUT THE AUTHOR

Missouri author, Richard Oliver Snelson has roots that are set deeply in the Crawford county area he writes about. The Snelson-Brinker cabin, built in 1834, still stands proudly in the Ozark Mountains located near Meramec Springs. Snelson was intrigued when he learned of the 1838 hanging of a 14-year-old slave girl who once lived there. Hence, The Hawksbill Crag, adventure novel was born. He has also written a light-hearted novel about the country music and outdoor wonderland around Branson, and for aviation publications. Richard and his wife, RoxAnne, enjoy living on a ranch with their horses, while he continues to pen stories of the Ozark area he loves.

Visit: www.thehawksbillcrag.com for pictures and history of the Snelson/Brinker Cabin and the 14 year old slave girl who was hanged for murder.